Undercover Love

by

Lucy Grijalva

LionHearted Publishing, Inc.
Zephyr Cove, NV, USA

This book is a work of fiction. Names, characters, places and incidents are products of the author's imagination or are used fictitiously. Any resemblance to actual events or locales or persons, living or dead, is entirely coincidental.

LionHearted Publishing, Inc.
PO Box 618
Zephyr Cove, NV 89448-0618

ISBN: 1-57343-002-1

Printed in the U.S.A.

With thanks to my favorite emergency room M.D.,
Jon Stanger, and to Sgt. Bob Fitzer of the
San Francisco Police Department.

Dedicated to the memory of my husband
Officer Bill Grijalva
who died in service to the
Oakland Police Department
December 15, 1993
Thank you, sweetie, for always believing in me.

Chapter One

❖   ❖   ❖

April Fool's Day

Lord, please let this be a joke. Julia Newman stood in her entry hall, taking another peek out the narrow window next to the front door. Nothing had changed. It still looked like a bikers' convention, minus the motorcycles, moving in next door. She was appalled but somehow fascinated by the long hair, ragged clothes, tattoos and bare, hairy chests. Despite her good intentions, she stayed at the window to watch a little longer.

The half-dozen men seemed out of place in the quiet, woodsy apartment complex on the edge of San Francisco's Noe Valley. She'd always loved the contrast of the rustic atmosphere in the middle of the big city, but right now it was the last thing on her mind. *All* of them weren't moving in, were they?

No way was she going to set foot outside the house today.

"Hey, Rick! What'd you pack in here?

Rocks?" One of them strained to lift a huge box out of the back of an aging station wagon. The man was in desperate need of a shave and a haircut. Julia shook her head. Her own hair fell to the middle of her back when she let it down, but his was longer.

A man with a graying red-gold beard and a bandanna rolled and tied around his forehead stepped over to help. "Rick had to make a beer run. He'll be back any minute."

Carrying the box between them, they clambered up the three stone steps to the small porch Julia's apartment shared with the adjoining one. Then she heard them trooping down the stairs inside.

The complex was built into the side of the hill, townhouse style, with the living areas at street level and the bedrooms downstairs. The unit next door was a mirror image of hers, and with every stomp of feet or raised voice, she could picture exactly where those men were and what they were doing. So far they hadn't awakened Poppy from her mid-afternoon nap, but Julia didn't doubt that any minute now the little dachshund would be at the door, barking hysterically for a chance to get out and bite some ankles.

An old but spotless white Porsche swerved into the lane and screeched to a stop among the other cars. Julia was awed by how close it came to taking out the bushes lining the drive without actually touching them.

The screech of his tires may have drawn her attention in the first place, but the sight of the driver unfolding from the car held it.

She wondered how such a big guy had squeezed into such a small car. He was well over six feet tall and wide through the shoulders. A black T-shirt played up his broad chest and muscular arms. Stone-washed jeans hugged his long legs and didn't leave much to the imagination. Wavy mahogany-brown hair brushed his shoulders. He looked almost secretive, with a full beard covering the lower half of his face, and a pair of Ray-Bans hiding the rest. All she could really see was the hard slash of his nose.

One of his friends poked at a cordovan leather chesterfield-style sofa in the back of an old pick-up truck. The couch looked too expensive —and tasteful—for this crowd. "About time you showed up, Rick. You're not paying me enough to move your furniture while you go shopping."

"Cool your jets, D.J." Rick's voice matched his looks, rough, rumbling... but somehow soothing, too. "I'm gonna put the beer inside. That's the only pay you're getting, anyway."

The men laughed as they went back to work.

Long hair, booze, and likely women, too. Julia frowned. This Rick person might be the type to catch another woman's eye, but she knew way too much about men like him. The neighborhood where she'd grown up was only a few blocks from here in the Mission District, but it was light-years away in socio-economic terms. She'd learned the hard way how to recognize trouble when she saw it coming.

Of course, she'd left all that behind. Now she had the security she'd always craved. She was a productive member of society, and she knew enough not to let a man like Rick trip her up. Watching Mama had taught her almost everything she needed to know, and she'd learned the rest all by herself.

Julia swallowed the familiar bitterness that crowded up in her chest. She let the curtain flutter back in place, disgusted with herself for wasting a perfectly good Saturday afternoon. There was laundry to fold, and then she really ought to correct yesterday's spelling tests. But she was back at her post five minutes later when she heard that deep, gravelly voice on the porch.

"Turn it sideways, Steel, or it'll get stuck. Oh, hell, it's gonna stick anyway."

Rick and one of his buddies were trying to maneuver the sofa through the front door, treating it as if it weighed no more than a folding chair. Julia could barely make out the words rippling across his T-shirt: *So Many Women —So Little Time.*

Of course, she thought with grim humor. *How charming of him to share his political views with the rest of us.*

But she froze as Rick glanced her way and caught her spying. Never taking his gaze away from her, he said something she couldn't quite hear to his friend. Then he shifted his end of the sofa to one hand and raised his sunglasses. Espresso-colored eyes crinkled at the corners, their teasing look belying the solemn expression on his face. Some faithless part of her mind noticed the flat, high cheekbones, the dark tan, the inviting thickness of his hair.

He winked suddenly and dropped the sunglasses over his eyes.

Julia's paralysis broke. She gave a solemn nod of acknowledgement—she knew better than to show any sign of being intimidated—and waited until he moved out of sight with the sofa. Only then did she back away from the window. "*Damn* it!"

That nosy streak was going to get her into real trouble one of these days. But it wasn't exactly nosiness… more like a healthy curiosity about her environment. It made sense to keep her eyes open, didn't it? After all, no one else was going to watch out for her.

She turned on the stereo, trying to drown out the thumps and shouts next door with Beethoven's Ninth. The music's strength and power suited her mood. When she sat down on the living room carpet and lifted Poppy into her lap, the dog snuggled close and grunted in her sleep. Julia ran one hand over her "baby's" sleek red-brown back. But her thoughts kept returning to him. Rick.

So what if he was tall, dark and handsome? You couldn't tell under all that hair, anyway, she told herself.

So what if his eyes had been full of understanding and humor when he'd seen her watching from the window? Her father had had beautiful eyes, too—at least according to her mother. Julia certainly wouldn't know.

And so what if his rumbling voice sent shivers down her spine? He wasn't going to get much chance to use either the voice or the eyes on her, because she planned to keep her distance. Polite —yes, of course; friendly—no, no, no.

Julia liked to sleep late on Sunday mornings. Poppy had other ideas. She pushed her cold, wet nose under the covers and nuzzled Julia's neck.

"Aaack! Not now." Julia turned away and curled up in a tight ball, trying to ignore the persistent dog. Poppy whined, then tried barking. Finally Julia sat up, pushing her hair out of her eyes and trying to focus on the bedside clock. "All right, all right. Oh lord, it's not even seven yet."

Poppy jumped off the bed and ran to the sliding door that led to the tiny, fenced-in yard and patio. She gave one more shrill yelp and waited for Julia to let her out.

"If you'd let me get dressed, I'd take you for a walk, you know." She unlocked the patio door and slid it open, letting in the foggy morning chill. Poppy raced outside. "Try to keep quiet out there. It's too early to be disturbing the neighbors."

That thought brought a picture of her newest neighbor to mind. With any luck, maybe she could avoid running into him on the front porch.

Sure. Maybe if she just locked herself in the house for the rest of her life.

Now she'd never get back to sleep. She headed for the bathroom, pulling off her flannel nightgown as she went. A pounding-hot shower helped put her brain in gear, and after a few minutes a comforting thought struck. He might not stay long. After all, like everyone else here, he was only a renter, and he didn't exactly look like the type to put down roots. Men like him never settled in for long.

Julia stepped out of the shower and wrapped a fluffy pink towel around herself. Steam misted the small room. She opened the door, then shivered as a blast of cold air rushed in. The sliding door was still open, and Poppy's piercing yip sounded in the distance.

"Oh, that little brat." She raised her voice. "Poppy! Get in here." Nothing happened.

She stomped to the patio door and peered outside. "Poppy!"

There was no sign of a fat brown sausage on legs. Where was that dratted dog?

She heard a growl followed by a whine, and her head swung to the left. Dismay riffled through her. The sound had come from the matching yard next door. The yard on the other side of the loosened fence board. That Rick person's yard.

"Not again. Oh, Poppy, you couldn't have."
Julia hesitated only a moment, then tucked the
end of the towel more securely between her
breasts and approached the shared fence, caution
pounding inside her head. She just hoped she
could entice Poppy back to her own side before
he noticed the dog was in his yard. She stepped
off the concrete patio and tiptoed around her
azaleas and fuchsias. Running one foot along the
base of the fence, she found the loose board and
pushed it aside as Poppy barked again.

Julia had to get down on her hands and knees
in the moist dirt to peek through the small opening. Lowering her head almost to ground level,
she squinted into the adjoining yard. She could
only see a limited area, but there was her baby,
calmly settled on the patio. And *there* was an
enormous, shaggy, golden... *creature* circling her.

"Poppy! That dog will chew you up and spit
you out," Julia hissed. "Get back here!"

Poppy ignored the warning. She growled at the
big golden retriever, whose tail wagged with frantic
joy.

"Get over here, you little—"

"Having trouble with your pet rodent?" The
gravelly words were followed by a deep chuckle.

Julia's hair stood on end.

She raised her head in slow motion. Looking
up, she saw Rick, his arms crossed over the top of
the fence, peering down at her with amusement in

the lift of his straight, heavy brows.

Her first horrified reaction was to reach back and pull the towel as far over her rear end as it would go.

Rick's chuckle turned into rumbling laughter. Julia closed her eyes, groaning inside. How could she have set foot outside her door wearing only a towel? What had she been thinking of?

As much as she'd like to slink silently back to her bedroom, all she could do now was brazen it out. She pushed away from the fence and sat back in a crouch, squashing her feelings into a tiny box in some far corner of her mind. Then she rose and met his gaze.

Rick Peralta had watched as his new neighbor's expression raced from white-cheeked horror to a mortified flush to cool self-possession. Now, with growing appreciation, he swept a quick look up and down her form. She wasn't very tall, but she was, well, nicely engineered. Maybe there'd be an unexpected bonus in getting stuck here for the next month or two. The sagging towel covered all the strategic areas, but it still gave him a good look at her legs. They were shapely, smooth and flawless, except for dirty smudges at the knees.

"Always was a leg man," he murmured.

"Excuse me?" Her voice, while gently pitched, was frosty.

"Nothing." He dragged his gaze above the waist. Her shoulders were slim and elegant, but she wasn't what you'd call voluptuous. Still, there was an inviting curve under the towel he wouldn't mind getting better acquainted with. Her face was fresh and rosy from her shower, and pretty without a trace of makeup. Lovely, he might say if he were given to flowery talk, which he absolutely wasn't. Her damp hair looked like tawny spun silk. Golden-honey ringlets were beginning to form in the wisps around her face.

Unfortunately, her mood didn't look so good. As a matter of fact, her wide, slate-colored eyes reminded him of a winter sky at dusk. She bit her full lower lip as self-consciousness and annoyance chased across her face.

Rick tried giving her a genial smile. But if looks—hers, that is—could kill...

Maybe he didn't have it quite right.

She cleared her throat. "There's a hole in the fence."

"Yeah."

"My dog seems to have wandered into your yard."

"I noticed."

She took a deep breath and spoke with strained patience. "Do you think maybe you could give her a push in this direction?"

"I could try," he said doubtfully. But as he turned away from the fence, the little wiener dog snarled and sprang at Shemp, his aging golden retriever. Shemp yelped, then turned and ran. Rick shook his head in disgust.

"Poppy!" cried the babe—*oops, excuse me, the*

woman, he corrected himself mentally—on the other side of the fence. He'd had her checked out before he'd moved in, of course, just like the other neighbors, but he couldn't remember her name this early in the morning. All that came to mind was her occupation. *Teacher. Third grade.* He wished the teachers had looked half as good when he'd been in school.

"What's he doing to her?" she was saying. "Please, don't let him hurt her."

"Not much chance of that," Rick said. "She has him on the run."

"Oh."

Shemp cowered, whining, in the corner of the patio. Rick heard a scraping sound coming from the other yard and wondered what she was up to over there. Swearing under his breath, he approached the little dog—Polly? It was something like that. When he got within a few feet of her, she growled.

"I don't believe this." He felt like growling, too.

"She's just scared."

Rick turned back to the fence. The woman must have dragged over a deck chair or something, because she now stood head-and-shoulders above the top, still clutching her towel.

"Fat chance," he said. "And if you think I'm gonna touch her and risk being mutilated, forget it. Come get her out of here yourself."

She frowned at him in indecision, then said to the dog, "Poppy! Get over here right this minute!"

Poppy held her head at a regal tilt and ignored her owner.

"Oooh!"

Mad or not, the lady looked downright delicious. But he'd have to be very careful in the next few weeks, Rick reminded himself regretfully. Too careful to indulge a wayward flash of interest in a woman he didn't know and couldn't trust.

Julia muttered to herself about impossible dogs and troublemaking men as she slid her arms through the sleeves of her velour robe. She belted it tightly at the waist, then caught a glimpse of herself in the mirror and had second thoughts. After yanking off the robe, she rummaged in her drawers for jeans and a T-shirt, unwilling to give him another excuse to leer at her.

Fully clothed, she ran up the stairs two at a time, headed outside, then turned to his front door close beside her own and rang the bell. She checked over her shoulder to see if Mrs. McCully, the world's nosiest neighbor, was watching from her kitchen window across the drive. Aha—for once she'd escaped detection. Mrs. McCully didn't miss much of what went on in the townhouse complex.

Rick opened the door right away. *Lying in wait*, Julia told herself. Then she had to press her lips together to keep from smiling. Okay, so maybe she was overreacting to the situation. So he'd leered at her—big deal. How bad could he be? He wouldn't have moved here if he were really the low-life he looked like. It was a nice, middle-class neighborhood. That had been her top priority when she'd been looking for a place to live.

"What's so funny?" Rick's coffee-colored eyes crinkled at the corners.

"Who's laughing?"

"You are. You're just trying not to."

Julia tried for another second, but she couldn't contain the grin that strained to escape. Rick's mouth quirked up in a one-sided smile. He leaned against the door frame, watching her. His old navy sweatsuit looked like a rummage-sale reject.

She hadn't seen him close-up before, no window glass between them, no fences. He was so big! Nearly a foot taller than her own five-four, she was sure, and his shoulders looked broad, his arms hard. Probably lifted weights. His size and strength made her feel small and feminine. Drat! She didn't want to feel feminine around him; she wanted to be a genderless, anonymous, barely-on-speaking-terms neighbor.

A flash of glitter caught her eye. The tiny diamond stud in his left earlobe made her think of the drug dealers who hung around the Tenderloin neighborhood where she taught. Her smile cooled. *Not your type, remember?*

"Come on in," he said, opening the door wider. Amusement still sparked in his eyes, but something else was there, too... some kind of observant wariness.

Get Poppy. Then get out. "Thank you."

Julia stepped inside and knew exactly where to go... after all, his townhouse was a mirror image of her own. She went down the stairs and turned right instead of left for the master bedroom. She tried keeping her eyes focused resolutely in front of her, but it was hard not to notice the only piece of furniture in the room, a large bed with disheveled black-and-gray striped sheets. Pillows were tumbled on the mattress and floor. The head of the bed stood against the wall her townhouse shared. Julia's own bed was just inches away, on the other side of the wall. Jerking her attention away from that too-intimate thought, she headed out the patio door with Rick close behind.

Poppy apparently had decided that things were getting dull. She nudged at the big retriever, who lay watching her. He didn't move. Then she backed away a few dachshund-size steps and barked at the larger dog. Finally the retriever reached out with one paw and clouted her on the head. Poppy climbed on top of him, yipping, and he rolled over, batting at her playfully.

"Poppy! Bad girl!"

Poppy stopped cold at the sound of Julia's voice. She scrambled off the other dog and curled her tail between her legs. A pathetic whimper started in her throat as she looked up at Julia, her eyes huge and soulful. Rick laughed.

Julia didn't. "You'd think I was going to beat her or something." She scooped up Poppy, holding the dog close to her side like a football. Then she turned to Rick. "Sorry we caused all this trouble. I keep complaining to the manager about that loose board, but he hasn't fixed it yet. I'll do something about it myself this time."

"No problem. I can take care of it in ten seconds flat."

"Then I'm sure we won't bother you again."

The retriever rose and lumbered towards her and Poppy. Julia reached out to pet him. "Nice dog," she crooned. "Big dog... but sweet, aren't you?"

"That's Shemp. He's kind of a marshmallow."

"Just a big baby." She rubbed behind his ears. Shemp whined and his tail swished back and forth happily, until Poppy snarled her displeasure at Julia's interest in him. "Stop it, Poppy. Shemp, don't pay any attention to her. You're *such* a good boy. Oh no, don't start licking me."

Rick folded his arms over his chest, but his eyes gave away his amusement. "Want a cup of coffee before you go? There's a pot on upstairs."

Julia wiped her hand on her jeans while she took a second to think. He seemed nice enough, now that he wasn't leering anymore. The thought of fresh, hot coffee sounded like heaven. The thought of sharing it with him made her stomach flutter. With anticipation? Oh, Lord. "Thank you, but I think I'd better take this little troublemaker home."

His expression didn't change as he turned away. "Whatever."

Julia wouldn't have wanted him to argue with her, but he might have looked a little disappointed, at least. Trudging back up the stairs, trying not to get her feet tangled with the retriever who stuck close to her and Poppy, she watched Rick's broad back. Directly at eye level was a really nice, firm—*never mind that!*

She'd never known walking up one flight of stairs could leave her so breathless.

At the top, he stopped and waited for her to join him, that quirky half-smile on his face again. "Guess I oughta introduce myself. Rick Per—" After pausing to clear his throat, he finished, "Rick Perry."

"I'm Julia Newman." She gave him a tentative smile. "I'm pleased to meet you."

His seductive drawl caught her by surprise. "Not half as pleased as I am."

It was the sort of remark she usually ignored. Terry Escalante, her best friend, said she took everything too seriously. But Julia found herself wanting to believe him. That way lay trouble. Instantly wary, she edged toward the door and said, "No, I'm sure I'm not."

She jumped at Rick's sudden laughter. "Ouch. Guess that one isn't gonna work. How about nice-to-meet-you, and we'll just leave it at that. Friends?" He extended his right hand.

Julia looked at it and tried to feel suspicious, but a smile began to grow deep inside her. "What do you men do, sit around and plan those stupid lines?" Finally she grinned and held out her own hand. *Big brave girl, Julia. He's just a guy, right?*

It was a mistake. She realized it the moment his large, warm hand enveloped hers. The heat of his touch flowed through her, and she wanted to leave her fingers against his palm longer than could be considered a polite handshake. She watched the humor dissolve from his expression and her lungs tightened.

Then Poppy whined and wriggled under her other arm. Flustered, Julia pulled her hand out of Rick's grip. He let go easily and looked away.

"So, uh, where are you from?" Her voice came out sounding ragged, but it was the first safe topic that popped into her mind.

"The Eastbay."

"The Eastbay?" she repeated, still half-dazed.

"I was born and raised on the other side of the Bay Bridge. How about you?" His expression was neutral now, that one breathless moment already forgotten, it seemed.

"San Francisco's my hometown."

"Mine, too, now."

"Right." How was she supposed to carry on a coherent conversation with the man when her insides were jumping around and she couldn't put two thoughts together? His rumbling voice vibrated through her and whispered up her spine. She wanted to close her eyes and listen to him talk for an hour.

It must be time to go home.

Before she could thank him and leave, he turned away and stepped into the kitchen. "Sure you don't want a cup of coffee?"

"I'm sure. Look, I think I'd better—"

"Hang on, I'll be right there."

She shut up and waited. Sneaking a peek around, she could see one end of the living room. As far as she could tell from her vantage point in the entry hall, the only item in the room was the leather chesterfield. Maybe he didn't have a lot of furniture, but what he had seemed nice.

"Ahh. I needed my morning fix."

Julia jumped at the sound of Rick's voice and turned back, trying to repress the feeling that she'd been caught snooping again.

He gestured with the heavy stoneware mug in his hand. "I may have been kicked out of my own house, but at least I was smart enough to take the coffee pot with me."

"Kicked out?" She'd suspected something like this, hadn't she? He must be some kind of a low-life to get kicked out of his house. And she wondered who'd done the kicking. A landlord? A woman?

A wife?

He started to speak but stopped, a speculative look on his face. Then he changed the subject entirely. "You know, I could leave that fence board loose. Polly could come over and play with

Shemp while I'm working."

"Poppy," Julia said automatically. Then, through the haze in her mind, the word *working* sank in. Work? The man had a job?

Maybe he was a computer programmer or one of those other jobs where people looked strange. Maybe he was a writer. Or some kind of financial genius.

Maybe he wasn't what he looked like. Attractive, sure, charming even when he exerted himself, but not what she looked for in a man. Not at all. Not the kind of man you could rely on, a man you could trust.

But maybe…

"Oh?" she said, keeping her tone casual. "What do you do?"

Rick looked her in the eye. "I'm a handyman. The owners hired me to help out the manager for a while. He couldn't keep up with everything in a big complex like this."

So much for the genius theory. "That sounds… interesting."

"Be sure and let me know if you need me to take care of anything for you. In your apartment, I mean." He grinned, and his eyes shone with an appreciative gleam.

"Sure. I'll let you know." *Over my dead body*. As she yanked open the front door, she added, "Nice to meet you. I mean, see you around. Thanks for putting up with Poppy."

He nodded and stayed where he was in the

kitchen doorway, sipping his coffee. The look on his face could have been humor or any number of other emotions. She gave up trying to analyze him and fled.

Smooth, Julia. She shut her own door behind her, feeling more stressed out from a few minutes with Rick than she did after a full day in the classroom. Her body seemed tightly strung. One wrong move and she'd snap.

He had long hair and an earring, for heaven's sake. He looked like a biker. His friends looked worse.

He probably drank too much and womanized, too.

He'd been thrown out of his house... and maybe he was even married.

His job situation was iffy at best.

No matter what kind of pull she felt toward him, he still reminded her of the men she'd grown up around, the kind she was smart enough to avoid. She'd lived on a street where half the houses were condemned. Most of the rest had been occupied by welfare families whose fathers had deserted them. The men she'd known were ex-cons, boozers, sleazy types who lived off any woman who'd take them in. They never stuck around for the long haul.

Remember how Mama always thought the new one was going to be different? But it never worked out, did it?

Julia had learned to be tough and fend for herself. She'd had to, to survive. But she'd fantasized about life in a clean house, with good food and new clothes and parents who loved her. Now she had it all, all except the loving parents.

And if there was one thing in life she'd learned, it was that a man like Rick Perry was born to drag a woman like Julia Newman right back down to the slums... if not worse.

Chapter Two

❖   ❖   ❖

Julia checked the clock on the wall and closed her time-worn copy of *Mrs. Piggle-Wiggle*, then glanced around the room. Thirty pairs of rapt eyes watched her. It should have been thirty pairs, anyway. Not all of her kids had super attention spans.

Several fiddled with stuff in their desks, watched the clock, or made faces at each other. One girl was busy examining the loving-hands-at-school springtime decorations on the east wall. She couldn't really blame them for being antsy this late on a Thursday afternoon.

Two of the boys giggled silently in the far corner of the room when one pushed the other's shoulder. Time to change the seating arrangements again. "André. Michael."

The warning in her voice produced guilty looks from the boys and an immediate cease-fire.

And there was Kathleen, whose head and shoulders were slumped over her folded arms on the desk. Julia frowned for a moment before she smiled at the class and said, "We'll read another chapter tomorrow. It's almost time to go home now. Does anyone have something special to share before the bell rings?"

A couple of hands shot in the air, and Julia let the kids go at it. Carlotta's parents had allowed her to take in a stray cat that had turned out to be in the family way. The kids looked forward to Carlotta's daily reports on the kittens' progress. Her mother had even agreed, in stumbling English, to bring the litter in for a visit once the babies were old enough. As an added bonus, Carlotta's own fluency with the language improved every time she spoke to the class.

When the dismissal bell rang, the listless Kathleen moved more slowly than the rest of the children. She was on her way to the door, the last one out, when Julia said, "Kathleen, can you wait for a minute, please? I'd like to speak to you."

Kathleen's eyes widened in mute alarm. "Uh... I guess so."

"Don't worry, you haven't done anything wrong. Come sit down." Julia moved to the half-circle activities table at the side of the room, pulled out a couple of chairs, and sat in one. It was child-sized and she didn't quite fit, but it put her closer to kid level. Kathleen followed obediently. She sat very straight with her knobby knees pressed together.

Lord, how the girl reminded Julia of herself at the same age: quiet, shy and intimidated by the world. Even the faded thrift-shop clothing seemed familiar.

The girl would need to find some hidden well of strength if she was going to get through life without turning into a perennial victim. But Julia herself was living proof that it could be done. And every time she gave one of these kids a helping hand, her own psyche took another giant step forward.

Where to start? "I've really been pleased with your schoolwork lately, Kathleen. You worked hard on learning those times tables, didn't you?" Actually, Kathleen was one of her most conscientious students… another similarity to the long-ago Julia.

"Y-yes."

"Good girl. But I hope you aren't staying up too late doing homework. You seem tired today."

Kathleen shook her head. "I'm okay."

"How're things going? Anything you want to talk about?"

"No. It's okay." Her eyes cut away from Julia's.

With a silent sigh, Julia resigned herself to keeping a closer eye on the child. "All right, but it seems like something's bothering you. If you ever want to talk about it, you know you can always come to me, right?"

"Right." Kathleen nodded. Then her expression crumbled and tears started to flow.

Julia's heart broke for her. She couldn't resist the impulse to wrap the child in her arms. "Sweetie, what is it? What's the matter?"

Kathleen sobbed something unintelligible into Julia's shoulder.

"It's okay. You can tell me when you feel better." She smoothed a hand over the girl's hair and back until she quieted enough to make use of a tissue. Then, as Kathleen wiped her eyes, still sniffling, Julia added, "Maybe I can help."

Kathleen shook her head slowly. "I'm just being a baby. That's what my mom said."

Uh-oh, thought Julia. *Step carefully.* "Why don't you tell me about it, and I'll make up my own mind."

"Mommy got a job. She's a waitress at a restaurant. It's a good job, and if she keeps it, we won't have to be on welfare no more."

Julia stilled the automatic urge to correct Kathleen's grammar. "Go on."

"But she has to work at supper time. She don't come home till it's time for me to go to bed. I get… scared, sometimes."

Julia closed her eyes until the dizzying sense of recognition passed. How many nights had she huddled in her bed, lonely and crying, waiting for her own mother to come home?

"Kathleen, tell me, does your mom come home right after work? Does she stay home on her nights off?"

The child's eyes widened slightly. "Yes."

"What do you do for dinner?"

"Mommy makes me a sandwich before she leaves. I'm not allowed to cook when she isn't there."

"What *are* you allowed to do?"

"Watch TV. Do my homework. Color with my crayons. I can't go outside unless it's a 'mergency."

"What are you supposed to do in an emergency?"

"Go to Judy's apartment. She lives next door to us." Kathleen sat up straighter, suddenly coming to her mother's defense. "And my mom calls me every night at six-thirty. That's her break time. My mommy takes good care of me, Ms. Newman."

Julia smiled. "It sounds like she does."

She had a legal and moral obligation to watch out for her students' welfare. Leaving a nine-year-old home alone for hours on end was technically illegal. But how could she argue with a parent who was trying to provide for that child? Where did the line stop blurring and become clear-cut? The mother was obviously doing the best she could with the resources she had.

"I'll tell you what, Kathleen. I'm going to write down my phone number at home for you. Any time you feel lonely or scared at night, you can call me and we'll talk about it. Believe me, I know what it feels like. Would that help?"

Kathleen's face brightened. "Yeah!" Then her smile faded again. "But what if you're not home when I call?"

"That's a good question. I'm going out for dinner tonight, as a matter of fact. You could try talking to my answering machine. Then I can call you back when I get home, if it isn't too late. Okay?"

"An answering machine? Wow! Can I call tonight when you're out?"

Julia grinned, pleased to hear the excitement in Kathleen's voice. "Sure. Leave me a long message. It'll keep recording as long as you keep talking."

"Wow, this is really cool."

Later, as Julia rode home on the crowded, noisy Muni bus, she resolved to monitor the situation. She wasn't sure she'd handled it right, but she didn't want to undercut Kathleen's mother's efforts to improve their lot in life, either. Julia stared blindly out the bus window. Her own mother had never made the slightest effort to provide for her needs. She'd always been too disinterested, too drunk, or too caught up in her own affairs. Affairs, ha. That was a pretty name for Mama's love life.

The men had floated in and out... men who never stayed long, men who always took, but never gave back. Charmers, snakes, street-wise types like that Rick Perry...

Julia sighed and deliberately straightened in her seat. Somehow, these days, it always came back to him. Rick.

She'd seen him hanging around the apartment complex now and then in the five days since he'd moved in. But he was usually gone when she came home from school. His car wouldn't roar into their shared garage until very late at night. Did he have another job, too? Or was he just out whooping it up?

The bus stopped with a jerk and nosed around an illegally parked car to get closer to the curb. Julia snapped out of her Rick-induced fog. She glanced out the window, gauging how many stops until it was her turn to get off. Not long; they were crawling out of the Mission District and into Noe Valley.

A seedy-looking bar and grill called Shelby's sat at the corner where the bus had stopped. Julia had never been inside. It was the kind of place that had its windows painted over in black, and motorcycles crowded into the dim, dank alley between it and the next building.

Julia blinked, thinking she must have really gone off the deep end. For a moment there, she'd thought she'd seen Rick himself, stepping from Shelby's side door into the alley. Another man— he looked a bit familiar, too—followed him outside. The one who might be Rick pulled a handful of paper money out of his pocket that looked as if it could rival her monthly paycheck.

With a noisy shudder, the bus pulled away from the curb, and Julia twisted around frantically for one last glimpse into the alley. All she could see was an arm wearing a navy-and-tan striped sleeve, and a broad shoulder swept by shaggy mahogany hair. Was it really Rick? Or was she just latching his face onto any likely male body?

And if it *was* him, what could he possibly be up to now? Sneaking around alleys… flashing big rolls of bills… driving an expensive car… and not working, to speak of. She didn't want to think it of him, but words like gambling, con games, even drugs, kept popping into her head.

It was getting absolutely scary, this obsession she seemed to have developed for him.

Bigelow, the apartment manager, leaned out his screen door and hailed Rick when he strolled into the complex late Thursday afternoon.

"What?" he said, letting his voice drop to its rumbling deepest. He'd been going all day, and still had a full night ahead of him.

"I got some jobs for you." The balding, scraggly Bigelow held his usual can of beer in one hand. After a week in the place, Rick had given up trying to figure out when the old guy actually bothered to work. He was damned lucky his brother was part-owner of the complex, or he no doubt would have been tossed out years ago. That same brother was Rick's ace in the hole. Bigelow wouldn't dare cross him.

He followed the manager into his cluttered apartment. "Anything for unit B-3? 'Cause if it isn't, you're on your own. I put in three hours this morning. Stuff you should have done months ago."

"I been busy. You don't know how much work there is to do, keepin' up a place like this."

"I don't want to know, either."

Bigelow grinned, displaying a broken front tooth. "But you got to, don't you? To make it look right and all."

Rick shook his head. "You're enjoying the hell out of this, aren't you?"

"Might as well take advantage of my good fortune." Bigelow's grin spread. "Matter of fact, B-3 has a little problem with their bathroom."

"I already told you, I don't do toilets." Rick shuddered. "Not even for B-3."

"You can't afford to be so picky. Anyway, you'll be pleased to hear, this happens to be a backed-up sink."

"Good. I'll take care of it tomorrow. There's no one there right now. I want to get in when Williams is home."

"Just make sure you don't do nothin' illegal in there, okay? I don't wanna get sued."

"Get real, Bigelow. I know what I'm doing." He headed for the door.

Bigelow said quickly, "One more thing. D-6 says there's a short-circuit or somethin' in her kitchen light."

Rick stopped. "D-6?"

"Yeah, and since it's right next door to you, I figured it wouldn't be no trouble at all for you to take a look at it."

Rick turned back to the apartment manager. "Is this something that just came up?"

"Well, she mighta mentioned it once before today. Maybe twice."

"How long?"

Bigelow swallowed and his Adam's apple bobbed at the look on Rick's face. He pulled open a kitchen drawer and groped around in it, then came up with a sheet of notepaper. Rick glanced over Julia's neatly-printed note. He looked up at Bigelow, disgusted. "You left a woman alone in an apartment with faulty wiring for *three weeks?*"

"Has it been that long?" His smile was weak.

Rick gave him a long, slow look calculated to strike terror into the hearts of men stronger than the likes of Bigelow. Then he left, letting the screen slam behind him with a tinny clatter, and headed in the direction of the D building. Dusk had already started to fall.

He grinned, his mood suddenly improved as amusement shot through him. So his "neighbor" needed some work done, did she? And she hadn't seen fit to ask him to take care of it, even though he'd invited her to. Times were truly bad when a woman chose Bigelow over him... especially a woman like Julia Newman.

She was a babe, all right. He'd started to dream at night about that sultry mouth. Reminding himself that she was off-limits—anyone who lived here had to be—had become a daily exercise. But that ice-princess look she usually wore for him, the one that announced *don't touch me*, was the most effective weapon of all.

His ex-wife had become an expert at that look long before the end had finally rolled around. The thought was enough to wipe the smile off his face.

As he approached Julia's place, Rick glanced in the kitchen window. It was a newly acquired habit, checking her windows whenever he passed by.

This time he stopped and stared.

Julia stood by the kitchen sink, reaching for something from a high cabinet. When she stretched higher, Rick's mouth went dry. She was wearing a pink tank top, a lacy little camisole kind of number, that strained against her shoulders and chest. *Nice view, princess.*

As if she heard the words inside his head, she turned suddenly and met his gaze through the window. Her arms sank to her sides. She didn't smile or turn away... just watched him, an unreadable expression in her eyes.

Rick wanted to walk past with a carefree whistle, but he couldn't. She held him immobile with a shadowed look that pumped him full of longing. He caught himself wishing he could reach out and brush the stray dark-gold strands of hair from her cheek. A shiver of anticipation shot through him.

Then the light over her head flickered and went out, and she jumped as the room went dim and shadowy. Remembering his mission, the real one and the current one, Rick shook himself and marched up the three stone steps to the porch. He stabbed at the doorbell... twice for good measure.

Before the last note died out, the porch light flashed on and Julia opened the door, her princess look firmly back in place. Her delicate, light-brown eyebrows were scrunched down. He tried to ignore her mouth.

"I wish you wouldn't look in the window. It gives me the heebie-jeebies to think someone's watching me," she said.

"Stand in front of a window in that get-up and I promise you, someone's gonna look." He wondered academically if she was wearing anything underneath the tank top. It didn't look like it. He checked again, and watched, fascinated, as the small buds of her nipples rose against the soft cotton knit.

The line between Julia's brows deepened and she folded her arms across her bosom as her face turned red. He'd already noticed how easily she blushed. Even her upper chest was pink. He wondered, if he ran his fingers over it, would it feel warmer than the rest of her?

"I knew I should never have bought this top," she muttered.

"Wrong. It looks great on you."

But she wasn't listening. Instead, she stared at his upper body, her expression gone suddenly blank. "Nice shirt." It didn't sound much like she meant it as a compliment.

Huh? Rick looked down. He wore an old long-john style shirt with long sleeves and three buttons at the neck. It was striped in navy blue and tan. Nothing to get excited about.

"What, this old rag?" He waited for her to

smile.

She didn't. "Well, now that we've admired each other's clothes, I'll just run along. I have some things to do." She started to close the door.

Rick laughed. "You planning to cook by candle-light?"

"I'm not planning to cook at all. Besides, there's a light over the sink. It's good enough."

"Hey, this is your lucky night. Bigelow sent me to check out the wiring in that fixture. Are you gonna let me in, or would you rather wait another three weeks for him to get around to it?"

Julia paused, indecision on her face. He decided for her and stepped inside. She stared for a moment, then shrugged and said, "Yes. *Certainly.* Why don't you just step right in and fix that light for me?"

"Good idea. I think I will." He headed for the kitchen, ignoring her muffled groan.

"Gee," she said from behind him, "it's too bad you're so timid and weak-willed. I *hate* having to make these decisions all by myself."

Rick stopped and turned around. She still stood by the door, a guileless expression on her face. He raised one eyebrow slowly. "Are you making fun of me, lady?"

Her lips pursed as she tried not to smile. "Who, me?"

He felt himself being drawn to her mouth again. *Dangerous territory, buddy.* His gaze swung around her, out the front door and then down the hallway that led to the living room. "Must be. The babe who looked like she was sucking lemons is gone."

Julia seemed helplessly torn between disapproval and laughter. Finally she grinned, a dimple appearing in her left cheek. "I give up. Go ahead and fix that stupid light. You might as well make yourself useful if you're going to be hanging around, anyway."

Rick thought maybe he ought to be offended, but he wasn't. How offended could a man get when he was looking at that dimple? No matter how hard she tried to maintain her dignity, it never seemed to take long to coax a smile out of her.

And he'd been smiling more than his fair share himself lately. Apparently she was unaware of the fact that women who didn't know him seemed to find him a bit intimidating. He sure wasn't used to being casually ordered around, anyway. "Okay, teacher lady—"

"Hold it. How did you know I'm a teacher?"

That stopped him for a second or two. He'd better watch his step. "Bigelow must have told me. Now, what seems to be the problem?"

She gave him a funny look, but let it go. "I don't know. It only works when it feels like it. I was kind of hoping you'd be able to figure it out."

"I'll take a look." He stepped into the kitchen.

Julia joined him a moment later as he fiddled with the light switch. "I almost dread asking, but have you seen Poppy today?"

"In my yard, last I saw."

"That's what I was afraid of." She sighed. "You'll never get rid of her now."

"Shemp likes her. He's teaching her to retrieve." Rick looked up. She'd thrown on a shirt over her tank top, and he lost interest in the dogs. Now the cleft above the lacy edge was shadowed and enticing. He doubted she'd planned it that way.

"Mind if I wash my hands?" His fingers felt sticky and he had a bad feeling his palms had been sweating.

"Go ahead. Are you thirsty? There's iced tea."

She took a pitcher out of the refrigerator and set it on the counter, then reached for tall glasses from a nearby cabinet while he dried his hands on a towel. "Oh—can you grab some ice out of the freezer?"

When Rick opened the door, he couldn't help grinning at what he found. The freezer was mostly empty. There were a couple of trays of ice, a package of chicken breasts, a small can of orange juice... and four cartons of ice cream, various sizes and flavors. "Guess you're kinda fond of ice cream."

She looked up, chagrined. The dimple reappeared. "I have some once in a while. Just hand me the ice, okay?"

"Yeah, yeah." As he turned away from the refrigerator, his pager went off. He reached for it, but not fast enough.

Julia looked up. "What was that?"

He yanked the little black box off his belt and glanced at the number on display. Someone downtown wanted to talk to him. "Nothing I can't ignore for now."

Her eyebrows started to scrunch down again, but she didn't ask any more questions. And Rick wasn't about to offer any explanations.

He didn't even realize how thirsty he'd been until he slugged back half a glass of tea in one swallow. Julia was doing strange things to his metabolism or something. "Thanks."

With one foot, he pushed a step stool from the corner of the room into the middle, underneath the light fixture. Keeping up a running commentary, he removed the big glass globe. "So how long were you going to let Bigelow slide on fixing this thing? You should have had an electrician in to look at it a long time ago. Or someone who knows what he's doing. Don't you have a father or a brother who can take care of this stuff for you? A boyfriend, maybe?"

He realized he was holding his breath as he waited for her answer, and he exhaled, casually of course.

"No." She blushed again. "And how would *you* like it if I asked if you have a girlfriend or a—a wife?"

Rick's fingers stilled and he grinned at her. "I'd be flattered. And I don't, if you're asking."

"I'm not. Besides, I'm perfectly capable of

doing minor repairs around here myself. In fact, I took that thing apart once already. It worked for a little while, but then it started acting up again. Maybe I do need an electrician, but I certainly don't need a *man* to rely on."

"Right. It might compromise your independence, et cetera, et cetera."

"I should have known you'd have a sexist attitude."

He'd started poking around in the fixture and wasn't looking her way anymore, but he thought he heard laughter in her voice. "No, I don't. I'm a very liberated kinda guy. But why should an amateur—of either sex—mess with this kind of thing, when there are so many people around—of either sex—who actually know what they're doing?"

"Beats me." Julia laughed. It was a throaty, sexy laugh that made him think of dark nights and rumpled sheets. Of course, everything about her seemed to make him think of dark nights and rumpled sheets. *You've got it bad, boy.*

He forced his concentration to stay on the work at hand. A moment later he said, "Bingo."

"What?"

"It's real simple. They put in oversized wire nuts. That's why the circuit keeps breaking. It isn't anything dangerous. But I'll have to find some new ones and replace 'em."

"Okay." Julia nodded, looking confused, and Rick wondered why she'd ever bothered trying to fix it herself.

With a laugh, he started to clean up. More to hear her voice again than from real interest in the answer, he said, "So you don't have a lot of family hanging around, huh?"

"Why do you ask?"

Her expression had closed up so suddenly that his instincts flared. "Just curious."

"I don't have any family."

"Where are your folks?"

"They died years ago."

"No cousins? Grandparents? Nothing?"

Julia shrugged. Her back was set stony-straight, but her face seemed... unsettled, and Rick decided to let it go. Now that he'd upset her, he wanted to comfort her, too. His arms itched to wrap around her shoulders. She'd lay her head on his chest and he'd stroke her back, holding her close. He'd kiss her temple, right where the stray strand of silky hair was coming loose from the pins....

Rick blinked. He forcibly derailed the vision in his head, but it wasn't easy. Once he had the glass globe back in place, he glanced around. Julia was gone.

He found her leaning against the open front door, lost in some world of her own. She seemed not even to notice his approach. An unwanted, unfamiliar empathy filled him. He didn't know what her problem was, but he knew that he, too, reacted badly to personal questions. People who tried to discuss certain facets of his private life learned the hard way to mind their own damn business.

He needed to come up with a distraction. Anything would be better than the mental retreat she went on when he mentioned the F-word, Family. And suddenly, more than anything, Rick wanted to see the sparkle return to her eyes. He wanted to see that dimple again.

He raised a hand to her shoulder and she came to with a start. Her eyes focused on his face. "Oh! I'm sorry. Are you done already? Thank you so much. Lord, I'm babbling, aren't I?" She produced a wavery smile.

This was the closest he'd gotten to her. She smelled like something pretty, some kind of flower, and suddenly it was his favorite kind. He'd plant a garden full of the stuff, whatever it was, when he went home again.

"Julia," he said gruffly. When he had her attention, he gave her his best leer, but it felt strained somehow. "Yeah, I'm finished for now. You be sure and call me if anything else, uh, comes up. I'm especially good with bedrooms."

His strategy failed. He'd expected to make her mad, make her laugh, maybe both if he got lucky. Instead, she stopped breathing and stared at his mouth.

Rick forgot all about the dimple and cheering her up. The pounding in his chest slowed and deepened until he could almost hear each beat. He felt the tension radiating from her in waves. He wanted more—he wanted closer—he wanted to run his hand from her shoulder down her arm, around her waist, across her back. Or into her hair, to pull out the pins and weave his fingers in the honey-colored silk.

The sounds of life around them—cars driving by, a dog barking, voices in the distance—faded. Julia seemed taller and he realized dimly that his head was dipping toward hers, while she'd risen onto tiptoes. His hand moved from her shoulder up her neck to cup her cheek. Her skin felt like warm brushed satin.

He met her gaze and realized her eyes were more blue than gray, much bluer than they looked from a distance, the hottest blue he'd ever seen. As he watched they drifted half-shut. His free hand slid inside the shirt she wore over her camisole and played over her back, pulling her just a millimeter closer. Her fingers curled into the mesh knit of his shirt as her lips parted. He thought he felt her merest breath whisper down his spine and to his fingertips. With his mouth just inches from hers, he could almost taste her—

"Yo. Loverboy."

The cool, masculine voice invaded Rick's sluggish brain. He spun away from Julia before she could react to the interruption, keeping her behind him, shielding her from view. He didn't think about it, he just did it automatically. When he saw who it was, he wondered why he, sharp kind of guy that he was, hadn't even recognized the voice.

His buddy Steel stood at the foot of the porch steps, long and lean, his sandy-blond hair tied back at the base of his neck. As usual, intense hazel eyes behind wire-rimmed glasses belied his casual words.

"Hey, Steel. Nice timing," Rick growled.

"I work on it, you know." Steel paused. "Are you ready to go? Or do you want me to come back some other time, like next week, maybe?"

"What I want you to do isn't fit to say out loud."

Julia peered from behind him. Steel gave her a dry smile. "Hi. Are you the Welcome Wagon lady?"

She tensed. Rick didn't have to see it, he could feel it. "Lay off, Steel. This is my neighbor Julia. Now get lost."

"Get lost? We have stuff to do tonight."

"Wait for me in the car. I'll be there in a few minutes."

Steel shrugged. "Whatever you say. You're the boss."

He ambled toward a shiny new luxury sedan standing a few yards away and slid in behind the wheel. Rick was staggered by the fact that Steel had driven up, parked the car, and presumably even slammed the door, all without him noticing. He was always alert—he had to be. When had he ever let his guard down like that?

Never, that's when.

He turned back to Julia. She rolled a bit of her

shirt hem between her thumb and forefinger, not meeting his eye. All of the bristling irritation he'd felt toward Steel evaporated. But with it went the cloud over his brain. He was going to stop this idiotic drooling right now. "You okay?"

She looked up, and he watched as her self-possession slipped back in place. "Yes. Of course."

"I'll be back to take care of those wire nuts."

"Thanks."

"Sure. I, uh, gotta go now."

"See you around." She inched her way inside the house.

"Yeah. Sure." Rick waited until she closed the door. Then he headed for the car, alternately lecturing and swearing at himself in his mind.

He saw the smirk on Steel's face and slammed the door harder than necessary.

"Got yourself something new going there?"

"None of your business."

"She's a looker." Steel started the engine and pulled out of the lane into the bigger drive leading to the city street.

"She's not my type." It was true. Most of the women he knew, good and bad, were tough as nails. Julia was just as strong, but it was a different sort of strength. And something underneath it seemed to bring out a protectiveness in him that he hadn't even known he possessed. It unnerved him.

He wasn't used to vulnerability. It made him think about other people's feelings, made him think about his own, too, dredging up memories he'd rather forget. Now if he could just remember he was supposed to be working, and keep his damned hormones under control...

"Not your type?" Steel smiled with real humor, something Rick didn't see him do too often. "You could have fooled me."

"Shut up and drive, Steel."

The blessed silence lasted all of about two minutes. Rick watched the road ahead of them, wishing they were in the Porsche and he were at the wheel. It was just as well. City streets weren't the place to drive off a foul temper, anyway.

Suddenly Steel swerved into a vacant taxi stand on 24th Street and slammed on the brakes. The car jerked to a stop.

"What the—"

Steel cut him off, his voice giving way to uncharacteristic urgency. "Son of a bitch, Rick. You didn't go psycho on me and tell her you're a *cop*, did you?"

Chapter Three

❖   ❖   ❖

When they walked in the door of Shelby's Grill, Terry Escalante gave Julia a long, hard look, but didn't comment. She remained silent as they found their way from the main room, the bar, to the smaller back room where dinner was served. And she didn't say a word when they sat down at a small, rickety table, after removing an overflowing ashtray and brushing off the chairs.

Half-horrified, half-fascinated, Julia took in their surroundings. Shelby's was every bit as dingy inside as it had looked from the outside. Flocked red-velvet wallpaper peeled from the walls, although posters of heavy-metal bands had been tacked up in strategic spots to cover the worst damage. The underlying smell was of age and frying grease.

Finally Terry looked up from her menu and said through gritted teeth, "Tell me again why we have to eat dinner in this hell-hole."

Loud voices, louder music from the jukebox, and the crash of crockery being slung on tables made it hard to catch her words. She'd obviously kept her voice low on purpose so the other patrons wouldn't hear her. They weren't the type you'd want to offend.

Julia glanced over to make sure the couple at the next table wasn't listening. No, the woman with the spiky blue hair and a ring through her nose was clicking her rake-like fingernails on the table while she glared at the large man sitting across from her. He was so busy shoveling food into his mouth that all Julia could see was the top of his shaved head and the complex tattoos on his bare arms. She turned back to Terry.

"I read in the *Chronicle* that this place is a little-known treasure." Julia blinked, then smiled as guilt nagged at her for telling her best friend such a blatant lie.

"It had better be good. Well, we both have to work tomorrow—at least we're guaranteed an early night. No way am I hanging around here for long after we eat."

They ordered cheese-steak sandwiches from a waitress wearing a "Shelby's—Hog City USA" T-shirt. The food, mercifully, turned out to be okay. Julia hardly noticed the lack of conversation. She was too busy sneaking looks around the place.

After she'd eaten her sandwich, Terry picked up her water glass, inspected it carefully, and took a sip. "Julia?"

"Yes, Terry?"

"The *Chronicle* was wrong."

"Sorry. But I heard the food was worth the lack of atmosphere."

"Oh, there's plenty of atmosphere around here." Terry wore an amused but impatient frown.

"I guess you're right."

Julia's nerves were shot from worrying that Rick would walk in. She hadn't considered the possibility when she'd had the brilliant idea of eating dinner here. And it was the last place she wanted him to catch her, especially after what had happened—almost happened —this afternoon. Getting caught snooping around one of his haunts would be so humiliating.

But she'd thought that checking the place out might give her some clue of what he was up to. Actually, she'd thought about nothing beyond Rick since he'd left with his friend Steel. If she hadn't already made dinner plans with Terry, she might have forgotten to eat.

Terry was watching her carefully. "What's going on? Something's bugging you."

Julia's first reaction was to deny it. But Terry understood men better than she did. Almost anyone would. Maybe she'd be able to offer advice. "There's a man."

Terry's dark eyes widened. "Finally! I've known you for—what? Six, seven years?—and you haven't gotten serious about anyone in all that time."

"This isn't serious," Julia said hastily.

"No?"

"He moved in next door to me. He's kind of different. I didn't expect to like him, but... I do."

"Is he a nice guy?"

"No. Yes." She shook her head, trying to clear it. Was he a nice guy? Life during the past week had been glorious Technicolor, while everything that went before seemed a murky sepia. Rick just moved in and turned it all upside down. "He's funny—he makes me laugh. And he's kind of smart-alecky, but then underneath he seems... well, every time I see him it's an adventure."

"So what's the problem?"

"For starters, he has long hair, and a beard, and an earring, and—"

"What is he, an artist or something?"

"He's a handyman. Or so he says. They hired him and gave him an apartment where I live."

"A handyman? You're chasing around after a handyman?" Terry smiled.

"I'm not chasing him. And he seems like an awfully odd handyman, anyway."

"What do you mean?"

"Oh, he's gone half the time. He has a lot more money than you'd expect. He just doesn't act like any handyman I've ever seen. It's weird. I keep thinking he hasn't been entirely honest with me." She gave a shrug. "Not that he owes me any kind of explanations, of course. I hardly know him."

"Hmm." Terry tapped her cheek, lost in thought. "What's his name?"

"Rick Perry."

"Do you remember my cousin Paul, the cop? I could ask him to check the guy out for you."

Julia frowned. "Terry, wouldn't that be an invasion of Rick's privacy or something?"

"Maybe... I guess. Let's assume for the moment that he's okay. Is he interested in you?"

Julia didn't answer right away. The memory of standing in the shelter of his arms washed over her. She fidgeted in her chair. "Yes. Maybe. It's hard to tell. I don't know if I trust him, anyway."

"You never trust any man you meet, Jules. Sometimes you just have to take a chance on a guy."

"I don't have a good track record as a judge of men's characters, you know." She'd told Terry about her one disillusioning relationship years earlier. *Danny Spinelli.* The name never failed to remind her of her own foolish downfall.

"They're not all like him. Or like your mother's boyfriends. I've told you before, you're letting a few bad experiences haunt the rest of your life."

"I don't do that." Julia looked away. It was an old debate, one they never really settled. *Don't forget how Mama always thought every new man was the answer to her prayers... but you know better now, don't you?*

Brushing aside the thought, she looked up and said, "I'm going to run to the rest room. Be right back." Besides the obvious purpose of the trip, it would be a good excuse to look around the place a bit more.

Terry raised an eyebrow, but didn't pursue the

subject of Julia and men. "The ladies' room is off the bar. I saw it when we came in. If you don't get mugged on the way, it'll be a miracle."

"I promise to be careful." Julia forced a grin as she pushed back her chair.

"And Jules?"

She turned back to Terry. "Yes?"

"I don't have a sexy neighbor. Keep an eye out for any eligible men while you're passing through, okay?"

"Here?"

"Well, if you happen to see someone who isn't into leather and chains..."

Laughing, Julia turned away and headed for the bar. But her smile faded as soon as Terry couldn't see her any longer. She must have been crazy to come here. What was she looking for, anyway? Some sign that everything wasn't as it should be? Just because she thought she'd seen Rick hanging out in the alley flashing a big wad of bills?

Give me a break.

She stopped in the double-wide doorway leading to the bar area for a moment to let her eyes adjust to the even dimmer light. Scanning the large, smoky room, she felt hopeless. There was nothing here for her to find.

Her glance skimmed past a broad back and dark, shaggy hair, then darted back again. Her breath caught in her throat.

Rick. Did she think it or say it aloud?

He stood alone at the end of the bar, his elbows resting on the long, scarred wooden surface, a bottle of beer in his hand. One cowboy-booted foot was propped on the rail at the bottom. He'd changed clothes since the afternoon, trading in the casual knit for a plaid flannel shirt. Then, as if it might have been too formal for a place like this, he'd rolled up the sleeves.

Julia told herself to get the heck out of there, and fast. Instead, she watched him in the mirror behind the bar for a heartbeat too long. She knew the instant he saw her, because his eyes narrowed and he swung around.

Lord help her now.

Several different emotions crossed his face within a second or two as he stared at her. The only one she could positively identify was the scowl that settled on his features and stayed. He nodded shortly and pivoted back to the bar.

So that was how it was going to be.

Okay, not a problem. She thought about skipping her trip to the women's room and decided against it—she couldn't let him intimidate her like that. The trouble was, she had to walk by Rick to get to the doorway where a faded sign pointed out *Rest Rooms.*

His head popped up as she moved past him. When she was about to step into the narrow, dark hall, he said, "Hey, you. Julia."

She stopped and turned around. He didn't say a word as she slowly stepped closer to him.

"Are you talking to me?"

"No, I'm talking to the wall. It's named Julia, too." His voice betrayed his impatience, though his expression was stony. "You can't go in there. It's already occupied."

"I beg your pardon?"

"You can't use the... uh, the powder room. Someone's in there."

"Oh. Then I guess I'll have to wait, won't I?"

He shot her a disgusted look. "Look, I don't know what you're doing here, but you might want to head out."

"What?" She'd known all along she shouldn't be here, hadn't she? But who could have guessed he'd react like *this?*

"Just go home." He shifted, seeming uncomfortable all of a sudden. "I'm sorry. But you've gotta get out of here. Now."

"Fine," she snapped, swallowing her mortification. Never let it be said that Julia Newman couldn't take a hint... okay, a heavy hint.

Rick wasn't even watching her. He stared past her shoulder. "Great. Just gr—"

"Who the *hell* is this broad, Rick?"

The low-pitched feminine voice brought Julia's head around. She stared in surprise.

The woman was about thirty, and as hard as they come. Julia could see tiny lines in her face even in the shadowy light. She was tall and wore the shortest shorts Julia had ever seen, with a matching jacket and knee-high leather boots. Her hair was an unlikely platinum blond, long and crimped. Her eyes were heavily made up and she smelled of cheap, musky perfume. This... this *person* eyed Julia up and down, then stepped around her. Resting one hand on Rick's shoulder, she let her entire length rub against his side. His brows lowered and his jaw tightened.

She didn't seem the least bit intimidated. "I turn my back for one minute to go to the can and you pick up someone else."

"Let it go," he growled, his knuckles white as he gripped the bottle of beer.

It was Mexican beer, Julia noted with new clarity of vision. She wasn't likely to forget a single solitary scrap of this experience.

"But—"

"I said drop it, Tiffany."

Tiffany? This is a person named Tiffany?

A few hours earlier Rick had touched Julia with the familiarity of a lover. Now he was rejecting her in favor of *Tiffany?* The woman looked like a streetwalker.

Tiffany shot Rick a petulant look, then turned to Julia, apparently seeking a more receptive audience. "This one's mine, honey."

Julia's throat unlocked. "He's all yours, if you're sure you want him. But he isn't much of a prize."

"Huh? He takes care of me just fine, ya know."

"I bet he does. Don't let me stand in your way."

"Why don't you just get lost?" Tiffany tossed

her hair back from her shoulders.

Rick's voice went deep and raspy. "Damn it, Tiffany, I told you—"

Sudden fury exploded inside Julia. It came as a welcome relief. "Don't worry, I'm leaving."

She pushed past Rick's hooker friend. Head up and back straight, she strode toward the door to the restaurant area.

Before she got there, she stopped in surprise. Rick's friend Steel sat with another man at a small round table in the middle of the room. As she met his watchful gaze, he shook his head almost imperceptibly and nodded toward the exit.

She had to force herself not to run.

But instead of following her instincts and heading straight outside, she walked carefully back to the dining room and sat in her chair across from Terry.

"Oh, my *God.* Was the bathroom that bad?"

Julia folded her trembling hands in her lap. "What are you talking about?"

"You're as white as a sheet. Are you all right? What happened in there?"

"Nothing worth repeating." She looked around the room. "But… do you think there's a back door around here somewhere?"

Julia shut off the alarm clock Friday morning and closed her eyes again. It was way too early to wake up. She'd lain in the dark most of the night, planning torture sessions for Rick, with his friend Tiffany running a close second choice. Through the thin bedroom walls, she'd heard him coming home in the early hours. She'd held her breath, fearful of hearing voices, too, his deep and rumbling, hers higher-pitched, of course. But there was nothing. Still, Julia knew the truth. He was every bit as low-down as she'd feared.

That sparkle, that inescapable magnetism she'd felt from him, had just been a mirage. She was probably right about him being up to no good, too. The whole set-up last night, the wad of bills Rick had been waving around yesterday, even the pager he wore, smacked of drug trade. Lord knew, there was no end to the amount of trouble a man could get into if he tried hard enough.

Julia hugged her pillow close to her chest. Worst of all was knowing that beneath her anger lay a heavy vein of disappointment.

She forced herself to get up and take a quick, hot shower. But as she yanked on her underwear, she couldn't help comparing her own small bosom to Tiffany's generous proportions, and she wondered glumly why she even bothered with a bra. She certainly didn't have much to fill it out.

Stupid thought. Bust measurements weren't something she'd paid any attention to in the past. Rick had scrambled her brain in more ways than one.

She fumbled with the buttons on her blouse.

Oh, what was the rush? It was so late that she'd already missed her bus, anyway. She'd end up driving to school, having to park Lord-knew-where, and still rush in at the last minute, temper frayed.

Julia wouldn't have thought things could get any worse, until she raced out the door stuffing papers into her burgundy leather briefcase. Then she stopped dead, shock bursting inside her and rippling all the way to her fingertips.

Rick stood in the lane out front, tossing an old tennis ball for Shemp. He looked up, his face going still, when she stepped onto the porch. He didn't even seem to notice that he'd made a wild throw, leaving the dog scrambling through the shrubbery for the ball.

"Julia." His voice was soft and low, nothing like it had sounded the night before, as he started to walk in her direction.

"Don't you ever sleep?"

"Not much." Rick shrugged. "I've been waiting for you. Can we—"

"You must be joking." Waiting for her? He had to be crazy to think she'd ever even acknowledge his existence again. She stepped off the porch and brushed past him, walking fast.

He followed her down the lane toward their shared garage. Shemp trotted along beside him. "I just want to talk to you for a minute."

"We have nothing to talk about."

"About last night—"

Julia whirled around. "Is there something wrong with your hearing?"

His body stiffened and he stopped, glaring at her. "Not a thing."

"Then *go away and leave me alone.* Okay?"

"No problem, princess," he said, his voice cold. "Come on, Shemp."

Instead of obeying him, Shemp nudged Julia's hand, trying to get her to take the soggy tennis ball and toss it.

She pushed his nose away. "Aaack! Not now, you."

The dog dropped the ball at her feet and whined. She looked up to see Mrs. McCully across the way glued to her kitchen window. So much for maintaining a little dignity in trying circumstances. Julia turned around and marched the rest of the way to the garage, swearing under her breath.

She was late, she was cranky, she had big-dog slobber on her hands. And it was all Rick's fault.

"It's your own fault, you know. Use a snitch like Tiffany, and she'll stab you in the back first chance she gets. She always goes for what's best for Tiffany." Steel leaned back against the leather chesterfield and stretched out his legs. He raised his coffee mug in a mock toast.

Steel was getting a lot of mileage out of the situation, Rick thought sourly. Good thing he hadn't been around for this morning's scene out front. "They all do. Anyway, she's always come through for me."

"Only because she owes you." Without missing a beat, Steel maneuvered the conversation right back to what had become his favorite subject. "So what are you going to do about the babe next door?"

"Nothing. She's out of the picture." Rick wanted to kick himself. He'd sat in that damned bar half the night, tuning out Tiffany and her constant whining, worrying about Julia's feelings. Her *feelings,* for Pete's sake. As if she were nursing a broken heart. Ha!

"Yeah, right. She looks like she's sitting right in the middle of it. And I keep thinking I've seen her somewhere before. Are you sure she's clean?"

"Absolutely." He'd stake his life on it. Even if she was meaner than a twenty-year beat man when pushed, he sensed an invisible core of innocence that she wasn't quite as good at hiding as she meant to be.

"Then you'd better keep her out of the way."

"Steel, do you think that after ten years of police work I might—just *might*—be able to handle this on my own?"

"You've been doing a hell of a job so far."

"Butt out. I have everything under control." He took a deep breath and hoped it was true. "Is this what you dropped by for? A lecture? I've got better things to do."

"Nope. I wanted to tell you I found a numbers runner who used to work for Darryl Williams. He's willing to talk to us, but he won't come down to the station. Said he could meet us at a bus stop on Eddy at three o'clock, though."

"Oh yeah?" Julia slid to the further recesses of his mind. "Let's hustle. I can't wait to haul in that bastard Williams."

Steel snorted. "Hey, I thought you and Darryl were getting to be bosom buddies. Didn't he send you a round of drinks last night at the bar?"

"You're just jealous." Rick grinned. "You wish you could be the one who gets to spend sixteen hours a day fixing clogged drains, chasing after snitches and getting cuddly with Darryl Williams."

"You got it, buddy."

Rick knew this case would be wrapped up soon and he could go back to something resembling a normal life. He'd never spent a whole lot of time at his condo in North Beach, but now the place was starting to look more lonely than usual. Stopping by every day or two to check his mail and messages wasn't enough.

The Williams case was creating an above-average amount of stress in his life. But he suspected it was due more to Julia Newman tripping into his life than to any trouble Williams might give him. "Come on, let's get going. We've got work to do."

It had been the Friday from hell. Julia pushed away from her desk and swiveled around in the rolling chair. She checked that everything in the classroom was ready for Monday, assignments written on the chalkboard, bookshelf straightened. Then she blew a few stray wisps of hair out of her eyes and stood up. Gathering her purse and briefcase, she headed out the door.

Now where had she parked that dratted car? Oh right, it was way over on Eddy Street. She sighed as she shifted the bags in her hands. Remembering she'd driven to school also meant remembering the argument with Rick this morning, and the scene in the bar last night. As if she could easily forget them.

When she turned onto Eddy, right away she noticed a group of men, maybe four or five of them, up ahead at the end of the block. They were hanging around the bench next to a bus stop. Her car was parked across the street at the corner opposite the men, and she figured the smart thing to do would be to cross right now. No sense asking for trouble.

Anyway, they made her think of Rick, with their long hair and beards and jeans and T-shirts. She didn't want to think about him anymore. She'd spent too much time thinking about him today—ever since he'd moved in, really—as it was. And he absolutely, positively wasn't worth it.

On the other side of the street, she hurried past a boarded-up storefront with two prostitutes leaning lazily in the doorway, reminding her of Rick's friend Tiffany. They giggled and whispered when she walked by. Then there was a pawnshop that was open, but protected with bars on the big front window and a folding gate at the door. Next came a garish-looking bar and a rundown apartment building. Clothing and bed linens hung from some of the windows. An old woman sat on the front steps, muttering to herself.

But in the alley two girls colored on the sidewalk with chalk, and they looked up and waved. "Hi, Ms. Newman." They'd been in her class a couple of years ago.

Julia waved back with an absent smile. Her mind was still gnawing on the problem of how to avoid Rick for the rest of her life. As she neared her car she wasn't paying much attention to her surroundings, and she missed the approach of three teenage boys, all hard-eyed and tough-looking, until it was too late.

Chapter Four

❖   ❖   ❖

"Rick. Take a look across the street." Steel's guarded voice intruded on Rick's conversation with the numbers runner.

Rick shoved his Ray-Bans up onto the bridge of his nose and looked. His blood turned to ice water, and he said a very dirty word. One foot, perched on the bench, hit the ground and he straightened, brows lowered.

"You need any help?" Steel asked.

"No, I'll handle it. Just keep your eyes open." He headed across the street, trying to control the protective reaction racing through him. Much as he would've liked to knock three heads together, he had to keep his cool.

Julia stood by the open driver's door of her white Honda, arguing with three young hoods. One was at the passenger side, another stood in front of the car, and the third had his hand around her wrist. Her face was pale and her voice sounded stuttery, but she stood her ground.

"I won't! Leave me alone." She tried to pull

her arm out of the tall kid's grip, but to no avail.

"Shut up and hand 'em over," he ordered. "Or you won't look so pretty when you wake up…"

The end of his threat was lost in a whoosh of breath as he went flying. Rick knocked him halfway across the hood of the car. Julia stumbled after him and Rick grabbed her arm, shoving her behind him for safety.

The kid straightened up, brushed himself off and demanded, "Who the *hell* do you think you are, man?"

One of the other boys pulled out a switchblade. Rick heard the click and looked his way, scowling. "I'm in no mood to mess around with you little creeps. Get the hell out of here and don't come back."

To emphasize his point, he planted his fists on his waist, sweeping his leather jacket out of the way. The gun stuck in his shoulder holster was visible to the boys, but not to Julia, standing behind him. The one who'd threatened Julia saw it first and his eyes widened. "No problem, man. We was just jokin' around with the chick, anyway."

The one with the switchblade objected to his friend's sudden capitulation. "Come on, Gilbert, we can take him —there's three of us."

"Shut up and get moving," Rick growled, and the one with the knife looked at him more closely.

"Sure, sure, we're goin'."

All three backed away a few steps, and then one by one they turned and ran, ducking down an alley in the middle of the block.

"Why, those cowardly little..." The rest was lost as Julia slammed the car door shut. She opened it and slammed it again, apparently not satisfied with just one show of violence. Then she leaned against it and covered her face with her hands.

Rick wiped the film of sweat off his forehead. He took a deep breath and reached for her, regretting the action when she flinched. Sure, he'd felt guilty last night and mad at her this morning, but he couldn't just stand by and watch her collapse.

"Julia." She didn't respond, so he turned her toward him and wrapped his fingers gently around her wrists. "It's okay now."

His hands slid around and cupped the back of her head. He pulled her against his chest, enfolding her in his arms, hugging her to him. She went willingly enough and seemed to relax a little. But when she started to shake, Rick was at a loss.

What was he supposed to do with a hysterical woman in his arms?

All he could think of was to stroke her back and croon words of comfort in her ear... so he did. Over her head, he glanced across the way at the other guys. They were watching him and Julia. Apparently nothing else on the street was nearly as interesting. *Well, let 'em have their show.* He wasn't about to let go of her.

After a few minutes, Julia stopped shaking. She leaned away from Rick, and he released her.

"All done crying now?"

"I wasn't crying. I never cry."

It seemed like a nitpicky point to Rick. Her eyes might be dry, but she was sniffling.

After opening her purse and digging around in it, she looked up. "Do you have a handkerchief, by any chance?"

He snorted. "Get real."

"I didn't think so." She tossed her purse inside the car, then leaned in and opened the glove box with shaking hands. Pulling out a tissue, she blew her nose. "That's better."

She slumped against the rear door and gazed up at him. Her color was still bad, but at least she seemed to be pulling herself together. "They wanted my car keys. They were going to take my car, and my purse too, I guess." She shuddered.

Rick felt something deep inside him tighten. He couldn't blame her for falling apart after a near-miss like that. But he wasn't used to feeling so shaken up himself. "They're worthless punks, but they're gone now."

"Thank you." Julia closed her eyes, then opened them again and met his. "Thank you for coming along when you did."

His chest expanded an inch. "No problem. I was just across the street."

"You were?" She looked up and eyed the collection of men at the bus stop. "Oh." Her gaze swept up and down the street. She shivered, even though the sun was warm. "I guess I'd better call the police and make a report or something."

Yeah, that would be just what he needed—two or three patrol cars cruising the streets and a bunch of uniforms asking questions. "Uh, I don't think it'll do any good—those kids are long gone. Besides, I've never seen them around here before."

She nodded, her expression blank, and hugged her arms around herself. Rick realized she was still halfway in shock and felt an unaccustomed tug of compassion.

"Come on, I'll take you home," he said as he shepherded her around to the other side of the car. He opened the passenger door and she climbed in without arguing.

He walked back to the driver's side and squeezed into the seat. After he found the knob to move it all the way back, he turned to Julia. "I need the keys."

She fumbled in her purse and handed them to him without a word.

Rick made an illegal U-turn. He stopped on the other side of the street and waited while Steel sauntered over. Then he rolled down the window and said, "I'm gonna get her home. You take over here."

"You want someone to follow and pick you up?"

"Nah—I'll call you if I need a ride." He wanted time to make sure Julia was really okay before he left her.

As he pulled away from the curb, he glanced at her. In profile, the lines of her face were clean and delicate. But she clutched her purse in her lap, her knuckles white. She looked so fragile, he couldn't believe she was the same woman who'd laughed with him yesterday, faced down Tiffany last night, spit fury at him this morning.

In fact, it must be a measure of her desperation that she was willing to get in a car with him today. Last night she'd looked ready to spontaneously combust. Rick closed his eyes for a second, knowing good and well he couldn't come up with an explanation that would satisfy her, and still not compromise the Williams investigation.

Damn Tiffany. Damn Williams. And damn *himself*.

He stopped for a red light and studied Julia covertly. Once again he felt the tugging need to see her usual animation. "How about if we stop and have a drink before I take you home? You look like you could use some fortification."

She shook her head and leaned back against the headrest. Her eyes drifted shut.

"A cup of coffee, then?"

She shrugged, as if it didn't matter to her one way or the other.

That was what Rick liked in a woman, an enthusiastic response. The light turned green and he stepped on the gas pedal too hard. The car jerked forward, but Julia didn't respond.

Then a vision of the inside of her freezer came to him, and he smiled. Keeping one eye on the road, he leaned down close to her ear and said softly, "Ice cream?"

Her eyes flew open and she pivoted in her seat to look at him, their faces only inches apart. The tip of her tongue skimmed across her upper lip. Rick's tongue itched to follow the same path. He caught his breath and swallowed hard.

"Ice cream?" she echoed.

He nodded.

"I guess that would be all right."

He kept his satisfaction to himself. When they found an ice cream place, he parked in a loading zone. Julia didn't say a word about it. She ordered a jumbo scoop of coffee crunch on a waffle cone. Rick followed suit. "You're the ice cream expert here. I trust your judgment."

They walked up the street with their cones. Julia seemed to be settling down okay. The tension around her eyes had disappeared, and her color was better. But Rick figured it was only a matter of time before she started remembering last night. What the hell could he say to make it all better? Not a lot.

There was a small neighborhood park at the end of the block. It was empty except for a couple of kids bouncing around on the playground equipment, and an older woman sitting on a bench watching them. Another bench stood empty.

He shouldn't say it. He knew he shouldn't. Hustle Julia into the car, get her home, get lost. That was what he should do. Instead, he said, "Why don't we sit down for a few minutes?"

"That sounds okay." She looked around. But rather than taking the empty bench, she surprised him by plopping herself down in the grass. Spreading her skirt, she crossed her legs Indian-style and turned her face up to the sun, sighing her contentment.

After a moment she glanced up at him, mild challenge in her eyes. "Come on, sit down. I feel dumb sitting here by myself."

He hesitated, then joined her on the ground, stretching his long legs out beside her.

Julia felt life begin to pump through her again. The terror and the helpless anger were fading. Much as she'd wanted to hate Rick, she couldn't deny feeling safe with him... grateful, too. It was time to call a truce, and he seemed willing.

She smiled as she licked her cone. The sweet, cold, creamy texture tasted familiar and comforting. No more unexpected tremors racked her body.

The sun was warm and the ice cream melted fast. She had to race to catch the drips. Rick laughed at her concern that she'd miss a drop or two. "I think you're an addict. Lucky for you it isn't a controlled substance."

She blushed, embarrassed to have her secret vice uncovered. "It ought to be. I watch what I eat all day long, but I can't go to bed without a dish of ice cream first."

"You carry it well."

Julia raised a questioning eyebrow.

"All that ice cream. It looks great on you." His

mouth quirked up on one side in that intriguing half-smile of his.

She grinned, suddenly happy with the world. "Five pounds less of it would look better."

"I never met a woman who didn't think she needed to lose five pounds."

"That's because most of us do."

"You're all crazy," he said amicably.

They worked on their cones in peaceful silence. Julia watched Rick out of the corner of her eye. So he thought she looked good. It was a surprisingly appealing notion.

His big hands looked strong and, even after the long winter, well tanned. They slid carelessly around the base of the waffle cone as he transferred it from one hand to the other. She wondered how they'd feel sliding across a woman's skin. Then she tried not to wonder.

He finished his ice cream first.

"You were biting it," she explained with a gurgle of nervous laughter. "You're supposed to lick ice cream, not bite it."

He snickered. "Baby, I don't need any lessons on when to lick and when to bite."

Unprepared for his response, Julia choked, spluttering. His words conjured up the exact images she didn't want to think about. Images of herself with him. Licking and biting. And no doubt a few other activities she couldn't even think of. A new tremor shook her.

Rick patted her awkwardly on the back. "Sorry."

He didn't look sorry. He looked pretty darned pleased with himself.

"That was a disgusting thing to say."

"I know." He grinned. "I'll change the subject. Tell me why you're supposed to lick ice cream, not bite it."

"In a minute." A rivulet of sweet, melted cream had dribbled onto her fingers and she took a quick lick. Then, before the whole thing flooded over, she whisked her tongue in broad strokes around the edge of the cone.

She looked up again just as she made one last, smoothing slide across the top of the ice cream, and she froze in place. Rick's smile was gone. The dark glasses hid his eyes, but she felt his gaze burning through her. His face had darkened, hardened. He looked as if he'd forgotten how to breathe.

Julia's fingers tightened involuntarily around the cone, crushing it. Rick flinched, then looked away, his lips pressed together unhappily.

Heat suffused her face. She raised her head from the ice cream and closed her mouth. "I think I've had enough."

"Yeah. Me, too."

She stood and headed for the nearest trash can, then rinsed her sticky fingers in the drinking fountain. But instead of rejoining him on the ground, she sat on the park bench this time, folding her hands neatly in her lap, trying not to betray agitation. Rick watched her in silence, making her even more nervous.

Finally she gave him a hesitant smile. "I guess I was pretty lucky today. Having you come along when you did, I mean."

"What were you doing on Eddy, anyway? That's a lousy neighborhood."

"I teach at Tennyson Elementary School," she explained. "It's a few blocks away from where I parked."

He looked disapproving. "Oh yeah? How many times have you been mugged so far, wandering around like that in the Tenderloin?"

"It's not that bad. Besides, I usually take the bus. There's a Muni stop right at the corner by the school. But I was running late this morning." She flushed, remembering why she'd overslept.

"Don't do it again."

She straightened, astonished by his abrupt command. "Excuse me?"

"Don't park on those streets around the school. It's too dangerous. Get up early enough to catch the bus."

Her hackles rose. Where had that high-handed, dictatorial attitude come from? "All my students live in the Tenderloin. I hardly think I'm too good to park there, for heaven's sake."

"So you're willing to risk another situation like the one today?" Annoyance streaked across his face. "What a stupid chance to take, just so you can feel democratic. Why not move out there and declare it open season on Ms. Julia Newman?"

Stung, she glared at him. "I lived most of my life in a neighborhood that wasn't much better, and I promise you, anyone who has a chance to get out *does.*"

She snapped her mouth shut, leaned her head back, and stared at the fluffy clouds drifting overhead. Where did he get off, trying to order her around? And where, a tiny voice inside her asked, did *she* get off, lecturing people who happened to disagree with her? Wasn't he entitled to his opinion?

With great pleasure, she stomped the little voice into silence. But, unexpectedly, Rick chuckled. "I rest my case." She spun back to him. "Why, you...! You're having a great time, aren't you?"

"I don't mind an argument now and then, as long as I get to have the last word," he admitted, the corners of his mouth quirking up.

Over her dead body. "Well, you can stop feeling so proud of yourself. What were *you* doing hanging around out there?"

Rick stopped grinning. "Me?" He swallowed what he might have said and replied gruffly, "Business."

"Some business." Julia sniffed. "And might I ask why it's okay for you to be on those streets, but not for me?"

"Because I can take care of myself, that's why."

"Okay, let me see if I have this straight. It's okay for a man, but not for a woman, right?"

"No, it's... oh, forget it. Just accept the fact

that if you can't protect yourself, you shouldn't go places where you're likely to be attacked."

"I'm not going to hide away at home to avoid any remote chance of trouble. I have a life to live," she said. "Anyway, your attitude is sexist. And you've already told me all about what a feminist you are."

"Okay, you can have the last word this time," Rick said. As she congratulated herself on how neatly she'd disarmed him, he added, "Just stay the hell away from Eddy Street, okay?"

Julia gave up. With a sigh, she said, "Can we talk about something else now?"

She tried her best not to smile. It would only encourage him. But somehow he made her forget all about wondering what he'd *really* been up to, hanging around in the Tenderloin with a bunch of hoods.

Julia insisted on driving Rick back, so he squeezed into the passenger seat of the Honda. She turned onto Eddy and double-parked near the deserted bus stop. "Your friends are gone. Do you want me to take you somewhere else?"

"No, this is okay. I'll find them." Actually, he'd rather have spent the rest of the afternoon making Julia laugh. He was getting pretty good at it, too. But duty called. He opened the door and eased one leg out.

"Rick."

He turned back to her. "Yeah?"

"Thank you again for being there."

"I'm glad I was." He went cold thinking about what might have happened if he hadn't been. Looking at her, he decided he liked her face arranged the way it was.

Then he noticed a tan spot near the corner of her mouth. Coffee crunch? Without thinking he licked his thumb, reached over and wiped it away. She stared at him in surprise.

"Ice cream," he mumbled, embarrassed. "I don't know why I did that."

His fist still rested against her jawline, his thumb only millimeters away from her lips. Suddenly, so quickly that he had no idea what she was about to do, she ducked her head and licked away the smear of ice cream with a lightning flick of her tongue.

Rick's whole body tightened painfully. He felt the reverberation of her touch all the way to his toes. As Julia's face took on a stricken look and she tried to turn away, he drew her chin toward him, running his thumb inside her lip, along the edges of her front teeth.

"What was that for?" he asked. His voice sounded hoarse to his own ears.

Her face flamed. "I... I don't know. I didn't think..."

"Do you know what it felt like?"

She shook her head slowly. Rick lifted off his

sunglasses and set them on the dashboard. Never taking his eyes off hers, he caught her hand and brought it to his mouth. Her fingers were soft against his lips, but he felt her tremble. His own hand was none too steady, either. When he spoke again, his breath feathered over her fingertips and she shivered.

"It felt like my heart stopped beating for a second." He smiled, a little rueful. "If you're going to do something like that to a man, you ought to know how it feels yourself."

Drawing her index finger between his lips, he nipped at it and then kissed it gently, soothingly. Julia stopped breathing. Watching her, he did the same to each finger. Her eyes clouded with suppressed desire and floated shut. Her mouth dropped open a fraction.

Rick had never been one to pass up a blatant invitation. It didn't matter; she possessed some kind of mysterious pull and he couldn't have resisted if he'd tried. He bent his head and lightly touched his mouth to hers. His tongue slid along her full lower lip and she made a tiny sound he almost missed. Her free hand glided across his rib cage and around his back, tracing an invisible line of fire. The inferno that had been banked inside him for days now blazed to instantaneous life.

With what few wits she had left, Julia sensed the moment the kiss changed. Rick stiffened and dropped her hand. He pulled her toward him with a rough gesture and she went along willingly, eagerly. Why had she worried about this? It was so perfect.

His tongue slipped inside her mouth. It started a slow, sweet dance with hers. His hands grew gentle and played over her back, but she felt the power he held in check. Then his fingers tangled in her hair, pulling it out of its loose chignon. A fireball burst inside her, waking her to the wonders of such a small intimacy.

Her nerve endings seemed sensitized. She wanted to touch him everywhere and hold him closer than she possibly could. His skin was hot, much hotter than her own. She could feel it sizzling through his thin shirt. Her muscles were melting, turning into creamy puddles. And she didn't care. She twisted her head, trying to take more of him into her mouth. She thought she heard him groan. A jolt of liquid lightning shot through her.

In the next second, his lips left hers. She whimpered, bereft, but he kissed his way across one cheek down to her jaw, tender little teasing kisses. Her head fell back as his mustache tickled her ear, making the earth move beneath her...

The earth? Or the car?

She sprang out of his arms with a startled gasp.

The sharp jolt of the brakes jerked Rick back to reality. *"What the..."* He sat up and looked at Julia's strained face.

"The car was rolling," she muttered. "My foot must have slipped off the brake."

"Damn." He glanced around. The Honda was

stopped at an odd angle a hair's-breadth away from the car she'd double-parked next to. Leaning back in the passenger seat, he waited for his breathing and heart rate to return to normal... to say nothing of other parts of his body.

Where had his trained powers of observation been hibernating this time? Obviously they went to sleep when she was around. As soon as he felt capable of moving, he reached for the door handle. "Julia, go home and get some rest. You've had a rough afternoon."

"I'm fine. Really." She didn't look at him or call him back this time when he grabbed his sunglasses and climbed out of the car. He slammed the door and watched as she pulled away.

He felt as if he'd been on an emotional roller-coaster the past couple of days. Shooting to the top when Julia was happy, plunging to the depths with her, too.

This thing was getting out of hand. He'd learned years ago how dumb it was to let a woman get to him. Physical attraction was a different story. That's all it was: lust, pure and simple.

But it was the wrong time and the wrong place, and he'd better not forget it.

Julia wandered around in a daze for an hour after she got home. Her lips burned, her skin felt prickly, and she kept tripping over invisible air pockets. Finally she fixed herself a glass of iced tea and took it outside to drink. Maybe the fresh air would wake her up before she became a real danger to herself.

She settled onto the cool, shaded porch steps. Sipping her iced tea, she concentrated. Sure enough, after a while she stopped thinking about Rick's mouth and eyes and hard, muscular arms, and started thinking about other things.

What in heaven's name was the matter with her? She'd been through all this before, and she ought to know better than to get mixed up with a low-life like him. *Maybe it's a genetic failing. Mama never learned her lesson, either, did she?*

At the very least, Rick could end up hurting her, maybe more than she could imagine. And at worst, he could be involved in some sort of criminal activity... stolen goods, drug dealing, maybe something even lower? When she wasn't busy being captivated by his rumbling laughter and matchless body, Julia had a bad feeling about the whole thing.

Sighing, she stood and brushed off her seat. Old Mrs. McCully across the way stepped outside with a watering can in her hand. She smiled as she began watering the potted garden she kept on the porch. Julia waved and started to open her door, but paused as an idea came to her.

Mrs. McCully might look frail, but she was the busiest, nosiest resident of the entire apartment complex. In fact, Julia tried to politely avoid her when she could, because she just didn't have time to stand around and listen to the elderly widow drone on for endless minutes about neighbors Julia didn't even know. But Mrs. McCully, who was home all day, might have seen things Julia would've missed.

So this time, she didn't run when the old woman stepped off the porch and headed slowly in her direction. "Hi, Mrs. McCully."

"Good afternoon, Julia. My, you've been busy lately. You've hardly been home at all, dear."

"There's been a lot going on—"

Mrs. McCully cut her off smoothly. "Except, of course, yesterday afternoon, when that new man was in your apartment. And I noticed you two chatting this morning, too. How nice."

Julia flushed. "My kitchen light—"

"He seems to be something of a handyman. It's really quite odd, isn't it?"

"I don't know, I'm not—"

"He keeps such unusual hours! And he's been spending time with that awful Mr. Williams…" Mrs. McCully's voice faded to a whisper.

"What Mr. Williams?" Julia asked, finally able to get a complete sentence out, even if it was a short one.

"Oh, that man over in apartment B-3, that—" She looked around furtively. "—that *ex-convict.*"

"And Rick's been—"

"Of course, I wouldn't want to say anything unkind about the young man… the handyman.

Not at all! After all, I know you're quite friendly with him." Mrs. McCully gave the slightly stunned Julia a sweet smile and walked back to her own apartment. "Nice talking to you, dear," she called before closing the door.

Julia wandered inside, dazed all over again. So much for thinking she'd pump Mrs. McCully for information! She blushed furiously, realizing that the woman must have been watching her and Rick on the front porch yesterday afternoon.

The door shut with a hard thud behind her, and from the kitchen she heard a faint rattling sound. When she checked, nothing looked out of place. And she forgot about it quickly, more confused than ever about Rick and whatever trouble he was brewing for himself.

She must be in really bad shape, she thought when she caught herself hoping that whatever it turned out to be, it was legal. As long as he wasn't breaking any laws, maybe she could cope with anything else.

Rick checked his watch. One-thirty. He hated coming home in the middle of the night, and this wasn't even really home. But since his bed was here, it would have to do.

He parked in the driveway at the end of the row of townhouses and locked the Porsche. As he headed up the porch steps, he eyed Julia's darkened doorway and wondered if she was home. A goodnight kiss might ease some of the tension he'd spent the night building up. Of course, she was responsible for most of it.

He unlocked his own door quietly. From somewhere downstairs he heard Shemp gabble in his sleep and settle down again. The heavy front door slammed harder behind him than he'd intended, and the walls rattled.

Then his entire body tensed and he strained to listen. He'd heard glass breaking—and the sound had come from Julia's place.

A window being smashed in the middle of the night?

Rick whipped his Beretta 9mm automatic out of his shoulder holster and slid a round into the chamber. Adrenaline flowing, he eased the front door open again. He made a quick inspection of the premises but couldn't find anything that looked irregular about her door, the narrow window next to it, or the kitchen and dining room windows beyond. Past those were the garages.

He was sure the sound of crashing glass had come from inside Julia's house. If someone had forced his way in... Rick broke out in a cold sweat. He didn't dare take the time to run around to the back and check the windows there.

He banged on the door, prepared to kick it in if she didn't answer... and fast. "Julia! Are you in there?"

The only response from inside was a wild

screech.

"*Oh sh*—" He stopped, saving his breath for the door. After backing up a few steps, he ran at it and aimed a good wallop at the deadbolt. The door didn't budge, but a piece of the frame tumbled to the ground. He was gearing up to do it again when the lock turned.

Blood pounded inside his head. Operating in pure reflex mode, he tightened his grip on the 9mm and stepped out of the line of fire as the door swung open.

Chapter Five

❖   ❖   ❖

Julia stood in the doorway in a pink flannel nightgown, hopping from foot to foot. She took one look at him and screeched again in fury. "You! I should have known! You call yourself a handyman?" Her eyes widened. "What are you doing with that gun? Oh, I've had it. I'm calling the police."

Rick ignored her. Pushing past the door, he stepped inside and looked around cautiously. From the hallway, he couldn't see much of the rest of the place, but everything seemed okay. "What the hell's going on in here? Did someone break in or not?"

"No." All of a sudden she seemed more embarrassed than angry. At least she wasn't screeching anymore. "No, nothing like that."

He gave her a hard look. "Are you sure?"

She nodded, her face turning as rosy as her nightgown. Her hair floated around her face and her eyes were heavy with sleep. Rick was almost accustomed to the jolt that shot through him whenever he saw her, but seeing her like this—fresh from bed and making no bones about it—nearly killed him.

He'd just started to relax and shoved the gun into his belt, when a quavery voice sounded from the porch beyond the open door. "Julia, dear? I heard shouting. Is everything all right?"

Rick hadn't realized Julia's full-blush capacity until now. At the sound of Mrs. McCully's voice, she went nearly purple. She glared at him, then hobbled toward the doorway. Without hesitation, she reassured her elderly neighbor. "Yes, of course. It was just a… a minor mishap. Everything's fine."

Mrs. McCully's eyesight seemed to sharpen as she looked Rick up and down, her chenille robe flapping in the night breeze. "I'll be happy to stay if you need me."

Rick almost laughed out loud at the thought of tiny Mrs. McCully protecting poor, defenseless little Julia from the big bad wolf—him, of course.

"No, I'll be fine." Julia turned her head to look at him for a moment. "Our new *handyman* just stopped by to help clean up a little mess he made."

"I did?"

"You did," she said firmly. After thanking Mrs. McCully and closing the door, she turned back to him, frowning.

"All right," he said, his voice level. "What is it? What happened?"

She nodded toward the kitchen without a word. Automatically he laid one hand on the 9mm and

inched through the doorway, then fumbled for the
wall switch. At least the damn wiring worked for
once. Bright light flooded the room.

Rick figured out instantly what had happened.

Overhead, bare light bulbs shone hard and
white, unprotected by the their usual cover. The
heavy glass globe from the ceiling fixture he'd
replaced yesterday afternoon was on the floor in a
thousand pieces. Strewn among the shards of
glass were patches of blood. A bloody trail he
hadn't noticed till now led to the kitchen door and
into the hallway. It stopped where Julia stood on
the outer edges of her feet, keeping the soles off
the ground.

Her mouth twisted in self-deprecation. Or
maybe it was annoyance at him; he couldn't tell.
"The light fell and I stepped in the broken glass.
My feet are bleeding."

"Yeah, I noticed." *And it's all your fault,
buddy. Nice job installing that globe. Maybe you
should have kept an eye on the work instead of on
her tank top.*

He turned around and walked out of the kitchen.
Before she could object, he swept her into his
arms and headed down the hallway.

"What are you doing?"

He didn't bother answering. God, she felt
good, her curves molding like warm clay to his
bones and muscles. Whatever complaints she
might have about her weight, he didn't have any.

Suddenly Julia seemed to realize where they

were going. She clutched at his shirt and bounced around in his arms, almost knocking him off balance. "No! Not the living room! I don't want to bleed all over the living room."

Rick stopped short. "Shut up and sit still," he growled.

For a few seconds, she obeyed.

He deposited her on the sofa and tried to straighten, but she still had a death grip on his shirt front. Knowing how upset she must be, and not knowing how badly hurt her feet were, he reached down to loosen her fingers carefully, gently. "Just relax, and—"

"Your turn to shut up." She pulled his face close to hers. Surprised, Rick let his hand fall away. "I want that gun out of my house. Now. Got it?"

She let go of his shirt. He stumbled, then regained his balance and straightened. Switching on a lamp, he narrowed his eyes at her. He wasn't at all sure he liked this facet of Julia's personality. "Cool your jets. I want to look at your feet before I leave."

"I'll be fine. Go." Her voice was controlled now, cool and uncaring. But her eyes… hostility heated her eyes.

"Look, whether you like it or not, I'm responsible for what happened. And I'm not leaving until I've made sure you're okay."

"I've been taking care of myself my whole life. Thanks anyway, but I *don't* need your help."

"You were singing a different tune this afternoon." It was a low blow. Rick knew it as soon as he said it. But he didn't really care.

She pressed her lips together, then gave a heavy sigh. "I don't want to lay eyes on that gun again. Okay?"

"Deal." He headed for the kitchen, feeling a bit huffy. There he was, risking his life—for all he knew—to save her, when she not only didn't need saving, she didn't even want him in the house. Of course, maybe it didn't look so good for him to burst in, gun drawn, ready to rescue her from a situation he'd created in the first place.

Rick slipped the Beretta out of his belt and laid it on the spotless countertop. Then he took off his jacket, threw it over the back of a chair and tossed the shoulder holster on top.

Stepping around broken glass, he pulled out a couple of drawers, searching for clean towels. After he'd found them, he wet one down in the sink and headed for the living room.

Julia was still sitting where he'd left her. She'd bent her knees and pulled her feet on top of her nightgown. There was already a blood stain or two on the soft flannel.

As Rick watched, she licked her thumb and scrubbed it against a faint spot on the oatmeal-colored upholstery. A bare echo of arousal teased him, a reminder of that sexy thing she'd done with her tongue and the ice cream earlier in the day. He tamped it down impatiently. The idiot was trying to clean the sofa, ignoring her bleeding feet. Women!

"For Pete's sake, don't you ever quit?" he said in exasperation.

"My feet will heal. The upholstery won't. Besides, the bleeding stopped. Hand over that rag, will you?"

Rick made a disgusted noise. Hanging on to the dish towel, he sat at the other end of the sofa and lifted her feet onto his lap. Julia sighed again—loudly—but submitted to his inspection.

He wasn't sure what to do. Did she need to see a doctor? As gently as he could, he dabbed at the blood on her soles, and was relieved to find only minor cuts.

"Hey, this doesn't look so bad, as long as there isn't any glass left in there. Maybe I should take you to the emergency room and let the doctors there check it out."

Julia made a face. "At this hour on a Friday night? No, thanks. Besides, there isn't any sharp pain or anything. I think it's all right."

"I guess you can always go in the morning if there's a problem. We should put on some antibiotic, though, so it doesn't get infected. And you'll probably want to take it easy for a day or two, stay off your feet."

"I'm sure you're right." Julia settled back against the arm of the sofa. All the resistance seemed to drain out of her. "I don't know why I was getting so hyper."

Rick's hands curved around her ankles and

over the tops of her feet. He had to force himself
not to stroke them in a more sensuous manner
than the occasion called for. *Down, boy.*
"Adrenaline. No big deal. I'll get you fixed up
before I go. Do you have a first-aid kit around
here someplace?"

She directed him to the medicine chest in the
bathroom downstairs. Passing through her bedroom, it only took him a moment to mentally
justify poking around in her top dresser drawer
for a pair of white cotton socks. He made a point
of ignoring the rest of her underwear—it was too
suggestive in his current state of mind. As for the
unmade bed, he tried to pretend it wasn't there. It
was probably still warm from her body.

But he did notice Poppy under the covers with
only her nose sticking out, snoring softly. That
poor-excuse-for-a-dog must have slept through
the whole thing.

Upstairs again, he lifted Julia's feet back on his
lap and smoothed antibiotic ointment over them,
gritting his teeth when she flinched. "Sorry."

"I'm fine."

Clearly, she wasn't. Her feet hurt, it had been a
wild day—Rick doubted she'd get back to sleep
any time soon. Then a brilliant idea came to him.
He slipped the socks onto her feet and said, "Is
there any booze in this place? Some wine,
maybe?"

She wrinkled her nose. "I don't drink much.
Wait, I think there's a bottle of brandy in the

cabinet next to the refrigerator."

He pushed her feet off his lap without ceremony and headed for the kitchen. When he found the brandy, he laughed. Nope, she sure didn't drink much. The bottle must have been a present left over from some long-ago Christmas. It was still in its dusty gift box with a red satin bow on top.

He found a couple of wine glasses on the top shelf of another cabinet and carried everything out to the living room. "This'll solve your problems, for tonight anyway. Maybe your feet won't go completely numb, but at least you won't care, either."

"And what's your excuse?" Julia eyed the two glasses with suspicion.

"I had a rough day. Okay?"

Her expression lightened suddenly and she gave him a smile. "It really has been the *worst,* hasn't it?"

Rick laughed as he settled onto his end of the sofa again. He broke open the bottle and poured a couple of full glasses. "Here. Don't gulp it."

"Don't worry." She tried a small sip, grimaced, then took another. "I know I'm going to feel better in a few minutes, but meanwhile, this is hideous stuff, you know. Do people actually choose to drink it?"

"'Fraid so." He savored his own. Just what the doctor ordered. After a few minutes he set the glass down on the coffee table. "Now tell me what happened. How'd you manage to step in all that glass?"

"It woke me up when it crashed. Obviously I didn't know what it was, Sherlock, or I wouldn't have stepped in it."

Rick went rigid with disbelief. "Let me get this straight. You heard glass breaking upstairs, and not knowing what it was, you just came tearing up here to see?"

Julia shrugged. "I'm a big girl."

"You're a fool. What would you have done if you'd come face to face with a two-hundred-pound drug addict?"

"Okay, I guess it wasn't so smart." She polished off her brandy and held out the glass for more. Rick poured her another couple of fingers.

"Next time just get out. Walk out the sliding door in your bedroom. Get help. But don't try to investigate on your own. People get killed doing stuff like that."

"All right, all right. I get the point." Despite the impatient words, she seemed calm and unruffled.

For what felt like a long time to Rick, they stayed right where they were in cozy silence. Somehow Julia's feet worked their way back onto his thighs. He ran a hand up and down her ankles. She finished her brandy and set the glass on the coffee table. He had another one and began to relax. She started to drift off, then opened her eyes halfway.

"Rick?"

"Hmm?"

"I'm sorry I was such a witch before."

"It's okay. I'm sorry about the light fixture falling. I thought I had it hooked up right."

"It wasn't your fault. And Rick?"

"What?"

"Thank you. I feel better. You were a big help."

"Heck, you needed someone. You were bleeding all over the place. Everyone knows blood stains are death on carpets."

She smiled drowsily. "Are you teasing me?"

"Yes, princess."

Just when he thought she must be completely asleep, she murmured again, "Rick?"

"Hmm?"

"Why'd you have that gun?"

He didn't respond for a moment, wishing he could give her a good reason. Her eyelids fluttered open. "Rick?"

"This is a rough town. I keep a gun in the house. It's not against the law, you know. And I have a permit for it."

"Mmph."

"I didn't say you had to like it."

"I don't. Too many bad people have guns."

"Which is why lots of good people have them, too."

"Like you?"

"Huh?"

"Are you one of the bad guys or one of the good guys?"

Julia's eyes were closed, her voice sounded hazy, but Rick understood that the question was important. He hesitated. *This isn't* Wiseguy *and you aren't under deep cover.* He did have an investigation to protect. Still, there was a fine line between protecting an investigation and totally trashing his own personal life. For whatever reason, Julia's good opinion had become important to him.

He figured he ought to be able to walk a balance across that fine line, for a while anyway. "I'm a good guy."

"Are you sure?"

"Yeah. Trust me."

Eyes closed, half-asleep, she smiled. "Guess I have to."

His fingers tightened on her instep and he wanted, foolishly, to lift her foot to his lips. He'd look pretty damn stupid kissing her socks. "Go to sleep, Julia."

"Okay." She dozed off almost instantly.

Rick sat there a few more minutes. But he couldn't stay all night. Finally he eased himself out from under Julia's legs and stood. After he cleaned up the first-aid equipment on the coffee table, he tackled the kitchen. He found the broom and swept up the broken glass, then wiped the spots of blood from the kitchen and hall floors.

Returning to the living room, he tried to decide what to do with Julia. He didn't like leaving her on the sofa, but he wasn't sure he could get her down the stairs to her bedroom without breaking both their necks. Crouching down on the floor beside her, he shook her shoulder gently and whispered, "Julia. Wake up."

"Um-hmm?" Her eyes didn't open.

"Do you want to stay on the sofa? I don't think I can carry you down the stairs. Can you walk?"

"Umm."

"Julia. Where do you want to sleep? I need to go home now."

"No," she breathed. "Stay." Her hands groped and found his shirt front.

"You mean you want to stay on the sofa?"

"You stay." Weakly but relentlessly, she pulled him toward her. Her eyes stayed shut, but there was a faint smile on her lips, those lips that always drew him against his better judgment. He closed his eyes for a second. When he opened them again, she was still there. Still sexier than she had any right to be. He wanted her more than ever.

But she was injured and half-drunk and generally untouchable. Maybe if she were conscious and knew what she was getting herself into, things might be different.

He could look, anyway. Her golden-honey hair veiled her forehead and was caught behind one small, dainty ear. Thick lashes swept across her rounded cheeks. And her mouth—God, that mouth!—made him think of summer peaches and plums, succulent and juicy. Just waiting to be bitten into. All he needed was a taste.

Red lights flashed inside Rick's head. *Trouble ahead, man.* He started to pull away from her, but it was too late. Her eyes opened halfway and, as she tried to focus on him, the tip of her tongue flicked across her lips. He was undone. With a groan, he covered her mouth with his.

It started out gentle, Rick in control, his lips playing over hers with subdued passion. Julia moaned and slid her tongue into his mouth, demanding a response from him. Her hold on his shirt loosened and her hands crept up his chest, resting on his shoulders and pulling him closer. Then her fingers slid into his hair at the base of his skull, and deep in her throat a purr started. Suddenly she was drawing him into herself as though she couldn't get enough. His muscles turned to jelly, then hardened until he thought he might burst.

She struggled, trying to roll toward him, and he eased his long frame onto the sofa, over her smaller one, never breaking the contact of their mouths. Blindly, he reached for the back cushions and shoved them onto the floor to make space.

With what little rationality was left in his head, he told himself she was overwrought, that she needed the human closeness. But as he settled on top of her eager body, bracing his elbows on either side to keep the bulk of his weight off her, he wondered who needed whose comfort more.

He felt as if he'd just stumbled from the cold into a warm, welcoming home.

Julia wrapped both arms around his head and hugged him close, her pelvis rocking gently against his. Parts of him wanted to match her every movement, but he forced himself to stay still. He was in this deep enough as it was. When he lifted his head to catch his breath, she tried to pull him down again, murmuring, "Stay."

"I'm not going anywhere, princess." He kissed her once on the temple, then moved to her ear, nibbling around the edge and pulling the lobe between his teeth. It was soft and delicious, her hair smelled sweet and—

"Ohh…" She stiffened. Then a bolt of pure blue fire shot through him as she mimicked his actions.

Her teeth ran delicately across his flesh and clicked on the diamond stud. Her warm breath caressed his ear. He groaned and stirred against the cradle between her thighs, knowing he was ready to explode with the passions clamoring inside him. "Go easy, baby… please."

She mumbled an unintelligible response and kissed her way across his neck to his collarbone, stopping to rub her nose in his beard along the way. "Mmm."

Rick was helpless against an onslaught of intense yearning. He'd never felt such hunger for a woman before, and he thought he might die if he couldn't have her. He needed to kiss her, touch her, feel her around him.

Laying her back against the cushion, he fumbled

with the row of buttons at the neck of her night-gown, his fingers agonizingly slow. Julia didn't help any. She squirmed under him and tried to tempt him back to her lush, hungry mouth. Her hands moved constantly, running over his shoulders, down his back, in his hair. But he was single-minded in his determination to succeed with the buttons.

Finally the long placket lay open. Like a man lifting the lid of a treasure chest, he pushed the soft fabric aside reverently. Her breasts were round and supple, beautifully shaped and begging for his touch, the nipples straining upward. He needed to hold her, to cup her satiny fullness in his hands. His head dropped forward and his tongue stroked one swollen tip. It wasn't enough. He massaged the other with a light touch of his thumb.

Julia's back arched toward him as she sucked in a harsh breath. She kicked her long nightgown aside and wrapped her legs around his. Moving frantically against him, she spoke, the words catching between breaths. "Rick... I... need you."

"I want you too, baby." His voice felt thick and his erection was fighting to escape heavy denim. He needed to be inside her right now, this minute, so much that it almost scared him. Levering himself up on his knees, Rick reached for his belt buckle.

Julia didn't seem to understand what he intended. She tried to pull him down, mumbling, "You come back here, Rick Perry."

Rick Perry. Rick Peralta's fingers stilled on his zipper.

This was something he needed to think about, not fall into by accident, no matter how painfully his body cried out for hers. No matter how entwined in his life she was getting. No matter how different and special she might be.

She didn't even know his real name, for God's sake. That narrow line he was trying to walk had become dangerously smudged.

Julia's arms wrapped around his neck and pulled him down for another kiss. He complied, still wishing for more, but the driving urgency had left him. Even in her foggy state, she couldn't miss the changed mood. When Rick raised his head, her eyes opened. He rolled onto his side, keeping her in his arms, his heart still racing out of control.

She looked dazed in the soft light cast by the single lamp. "Wh-what's the matter?"

"I think… maybe we want to think about this first." It was the only thing he could come up with. Perspiration trickled down his temple. His brain felt like oatmeal, but his body remained on full alert. How could he have let it go so far, so fast?

Julia's eyes widened. "You don't want to? I mean, you can stop just like that?"

When she turned away from him and started to pull out of his arms, he tightened them around her. "Don't go. I want to hold you." Next best would have to do for now.

Her head snapped around and the look of devastation on her face arrowed straight to his gut. "But you don't want to... you stopped..."

"Is that what you're thinking? That I don't want you? Think again, princess." The ache in his groin testified to his wanting her, all right. "But maybe you don't want to rush into this."

Confusion replaced her hurt look, and she buried her face against his neck. When she exhaled, the warm gust tickled his flesh, sending another current of desire coursing through him. Her voice was muffled and breathy. "That's the nicest thing anyone ever did for me."

Guilt filled him, and he wished he *had* been putting her needs first. Obviously, no one else had for a long time.

What he really ought to do was pack up and get out. That would be an intelligent response to the situation. Instead, he stayed. The comfort of her body was worth the cost to his soul. He felt someone's heart beating—he couldn't tell if it was hers or his own—and after a few painful minutes, its pace slowed. Eventually, relaxation and an unnatural contentment overtook him.

It was close to dawn when Rick opened his eyes again. He jerked awake and almost fell off the sofa. "Goddammit."

Julia sat up and rubbed her eyes, mumbling to

herself.

"I've gotta go."

"Unh."

"Do you need help getting down the stairs?"
Oh *great,* he thought. That was what had gotten
him into trouble in the first place.

"Unh... no. Okay. I'm okay."

She didn't sound quite all there. Rick parked
himself on the opposite end of the sofa. "Are you
awake?"

"Yes. I'll be fine." Her voice was getting
stronger. She looked his way, her eyes luminous
in the dim light. "Thank you for everything. And
I'm sorry about... what happened before. Thank
you for being a gentleman about it."

Rick Peralta... a gentleman? It wasn't something he'd been accused of too often. He thought
about leaning over and giving her a goodnight
kiss before he left, then thought better of it.

Halfway down the hall, he stopped and turned
back to her. "Julia."

She raised questioning eyes at his tone.
"What?"

"I'll stop by tomorrow." He took a deep breath.
"It's late now, but we need to talk. Okay?"

"Okay. Yes." She stood up and followed him
slowly to the door. Before he left, he grasped the
back of her head and gave her a brief, hard kiss.
Then, before he could forget himself again, he
walked out. He waited on the porch until he heard
the door lock.

Back in his own place, he closed the door carefully and let his breath out in a whoosh. What was it about Julia that turned him into some kind of a wild man he didn't recognize? Where was his usual cool self, who didn't get worked up about any woman?

Apparently it was different with this one. And he was going to go nuts if he had to stay in this place another day and not touch her.

Chapter Six

❖   ❖   ❖

Julia slept late on Saturday morning. As she started to drift awake, visions of the previous night's events flashed inside her head and her eyes flew open. For once in her life she woke up instantly. "Oh no!"

She couldn't have behaved like such a slut, could she? She'd sworn years ago that her life would never be a repeat of her mother's. And yet there she'd been, about as close as she could get to making love with a man she'd known less than a week.

Don't forget how Mama always let herself be carried away by the moment. She never once stopped to think about consequences, did she?

But this was different. Rick had been so protective, so concerned. She'd never seen such a rough, tough man who could still show such gentleness.

Julia shook her head. Time to get up, before she was positively wallowing in Rick's better qualities. She threw her legs over the edge of the mattress, stood up and squeaked. Rolling onto the sides of her feet, she hobbled upstairs.

All signs of her accident last night had disappeared from the entry hall and kitchen. Rick must have cleaned up the broken glass and blood. Overhead were two bare bulbs. Besides the wire nuts he'd talked about fixing, that globe would have to be replaced now, too.

Julia had just fixed herself a cup of strong coffee when the doorbell rang. Who'd be at the door at ten o'clock on a Saturday morning?

When she thought about it, her heart started to pound. She got up and tottered to the front door as fast as her burning feet would carry her. It was the paper boy. She paid him off and shut the door, then leaned her forehead against the cool wooden surface.

This is ridiculous. So Rick wanted to sleep with you. It doesn't mean he's going to fall at your feet.

But he said he'd come by today, didn't he?

A foggy memory of his murmured words filled her head. If he insisted on continuing to hang around, she was beginning to think that maybe she wouldn't mind.

She hobbled down the stairs to her bedroom and pulled a teal sweatshirt and matching pants out of a drawer. When she looked in the bathroom mirror, she nearly screamed. Thank God it had been the paper boy at the door, not Rick.

An hour later, looking and feeling more human, Julia was settled on the sofa watching Audrey Hepburn and Humphrey Bogart fall in love. Poppy climbed into her lap, sniffing at the popcorn she'd fixed for breakfast. Julia absent-mindedly pushed the dog's nose away from the bowl.

It was a good thing she'd already seen the movie, because she spent most of it worrying about whether she was falling too hard, too fast, for a man who seemed totally unsuitable for her. An ominous sense of *déjà vu* haunted her, but the warmth in her heart almost overshadowed the clutch of fear in her belly.

Halfway through the movie, and a dozen times through different possible constructions on Rick's true character, there was a sharp rap at the door. *Great,* Julia thought as she got up, *this time it'll be the mail carrier.* Tension vibrated through her just the same.

It wasn't the mail carrier. It was Rick. He carried a bulky plastic shopping bag in each hand, and his expression was tentative. Julia forgot everything she ought to ask him. He seemed similarly struck dumb. The big-city noises in the background faded away, leaving greenery rustling in the slight breeze the only sounds she heard. Finally she managed to say, "Hi."

He took off his sunglasses and smiled, and Julia was transfixed. Every moment of the passion they'd shared last night was packed into that intimate look. His eyes crinkled at the corners and his brow lightened. She swallowed.

His beard didn't seem as scruffy as it used to.

She wondered what he would look like without it. The sight of his diamond earring brought a sudden memory of drawing his ear lobe between her teeth. His helpless groan. The hot, hard pressure of him between her legs, and the fire that had blazed through her, feeling the effect she had on him...

Oh, Lord. Stop!

When Rick spoke, his voice was as smooth as satin sheets, and wrapped around her just as silkily. It was nothing like his usual growl. "How are you feeling this morning?"

"Fine. Thank you."

"Your feet are better? No bleeding?" He looked down at her clean white socks.

"They're okay. Thank you for everything you did for me last night." As soon as the words were out, she wished them back. "I mean, I wasn't talking about... oh, never mind."

A slow grin spread across Rick's face. "I wasn't expecting any thanks." As Julia blushed predictably, he added, "Can I come in?"

"Yes, of course." She opened the door all the way and ushered him inside. In the living room, she switched off the television. The floor was littered with popcorn. A guilt-stricken Poppy eyed Julia.

She sighed, ignoring Rick's snort of laughter. "One of these days, Poppy. Just you wait and see." After scooping the mess back into the bowl, she turned to Rick and smiled. "Don't blame me for her manners. Would you like a cup of coffee?"

He dropped the bags on a side chair. "That'd be great."

"Have a seat. I'll be right back."

"Let me get it. You shouldn't be on your feet, anyway." He followed her into the kitchen and ordered, "Sit down. And put your feet up on the other chair."

She emptied the popcorn into the trash, then sat. "The mugs are in the cabinet over the coffee-maker."

"Thanks. Have you had breakfast yet?" She started to respond, but he interrupted. "And popcorn doesn't count."

Julia laughed. "All right then, no, I haven't."

"How about if I fix us something?"

Hey, I could get used to this kind of treatment pretty easily. Smiling, she warned, "There isn't much food in the house."

"I came prepared." Rick went back to the living room and returned with the two plastic bags. He put them on the counter and pulled a package of bacon, a chunk of cheddar cheese and some small red potatoes out of one of them. "Now let's see what there is to work with." Julia watched wide-eyed as he poked around in the refrigerator, coming up with an assortment of wilted-looking vegetables. "Hey, you have great stuff in here."

"I do?"

"Sure. We're gonna eat like royalty."

"Whatever you say." She couldn't imagine

what he had in mind for breakfast, but she was content to watch him work. Once in a while she had to direct him to a cabinet for a frying pan, or to a drawer for the grater. Mostly he chopped vegetables and talked to her, teased her, made her feel like an old friend.

Breakfast was ready before she would have thought. Julia looked at her plate. On it sat a mound of sautéed onions, peppers, mushrooms, zucchini and tomatoes mixed with fried potatoes and bacon. Cheese was melted all over the top.

She admired his artwork. "I don't know what you call this, but it looks wonderful."

"My mother calls it a mess, but she eats it just the same. When she can talk me into cooking for her, that is."

"You're a man of hidden talents," Julia said, repressing a smile.

He eyed her suspiciously. "What's that look for?"

"I'm trying to imagine you with a doting mother."

"Any luck?"

"No-o-o." She tried to picture him as a small, delicate child, and failed.

"Just as well." Rick winked. "She's forgotten how to dote. Right now, she's in Irian Jaya for a month. My dad, too."

"I've never heard of it."

"It's the other side of Indonesia. The jungle's full of tribes that claim they don't practice canni-balism anymore. That's where my folks are hanging out."

Julia was totally confused. Were they some kind of missionaries? "But... why?"

"Adventure, I guess. Life in the Bay Area must be too tame for them." He grinned.

"They sound like very interesting people." Privately, she thought they sounded like very *odd* people, but they were his parents, after all. At least he was fortunate enough to have parents.

She took a bite of breakfast. "Mmm! It *is* wonderful."

"My mother never lies."

"Of course not, but she might... I mean... well, try to protect your feelings or something. If you cooked something really awful, that is."

Rick's heavy, dark brows lowered into a frown. "Do I look like the type who needs to be coddled?"

Smiling, she shook her head. "No. But everyone needs a little coddling now and then."

"I'll have to remember you said that." His expression broke into a smug smile. "Everyone needs a little cuddling now and then."

Julia laughed out loud. "That's *coddling,* mister, not *cuddling.*"

She couldn't believe how quickly she'd fallen into the rhythm of easy conversation with Rick. He managed to move seamlessly from bad humor to good, from serious subjects to sexual innuendo to just plain teasing. She doubted she'd have been able to keep up with him a week ago, but she was catching on fast—and enjoying it.

When he'd finished eating, Rick laid down his

fork. "I almost forgot to tell you." Nodding toward the other plastic bag still sitting on the counter, he said, "I ran by the hardware store this morning. Got everything to fix the kitchen light. As soon as I clean up here, I'll take care of it."

"That was quick."

His gaze went back to his plate. "I'm not used to screwing things up so badly." A faint ribbon of red burned across his cheeks as he pushed back his chair and got up from the table.

Julia was enchanted. "Don't tell me your Male Ego is bruised."

"It isn't," he growled. "I just wanna get the job done right. And you don't have to look so damn pleased."

"Okay. But I'll be sure and tell Mr. Bigelow what good work you're doing."

"Don't push me, lady." He carried their plates to the sink and turned on the water.

"Oh, come on. So you made a mistake. We all do it." She stood up. "Please don't worry about the dishes. You cooked the meal. I'll take care of the clean-up."

"Sit down. I'll do it." His tone brooked no argument. She sat, relieved underneath it all to be off her feet. He went on, "And a mistake isn't the same thing as a *stupid* mistake. You could have been hurt a lot worse than you were."

Julia was unaccustomed to having anyone else take responsibility for her health and welfare. Touched by his concern, she said, "Stop blaming yourself. The real dummy was me, tramping around barefoot in broken glass. My only excuse is that I was maybe one-quarter awake."

Rick looked up with a grin. "I think I like you that way."

Her stomach dropped at his not-so-subtle reminder, and the memories rushed over her again, heating her blood. Her mind may have been half-asleep, but her body had been going full steam ahead, hadn't it? It was breaking every rule she'd ever set for herself. She squared her shoulders. "Rick... don't ever give me brandy again. I think I'm allergic to it."

He smiled as he filled the frying pan with soapy water. "Don't ever grab me and beg me to stay again." His smile faded and his eyes closed. Then he opened them and glared at her. "Next time I will."

"I didn't."

"You did."

She wrinkled her nose. "Oh, Lord. I did, didn't I?"

"Yup."

"That wasn't the real me," Julia said earnestly. "I don't fall into bed with just anyone—I mean, I only—oh, never mind," she finished as embarrassment flooded through her.

"I know." For once Rick didn't laugh, surprising her. He dropped the dishcloth into the sink and walked over to the dinette table, coming to a halt right in front of her.

She stopped breathing and waited to see what he intended. When he placed a hand on her shoulder, a shiver ran through her. It intensified as his thumb stroked a circle on the side of her neck. His eyes softened, the espresso color warming and deepening.

She could lose herself in those eyes. How could she ever have distrusted him? No one who looked at her like that could possibly mean to hurt her.

"We need to talk, princess. About us."

"Yes." It came out a whispered sigh; she couldn't manage anything more.

"There are things you don't know about me."

Her instincts started beeping at her. "Like what?"

Rick watched Julia straighten in the dinette chair. He hesitated, indecisive for once. But one way or another, this thing between them had to be settled.

They'd reached a fork in the road. In one direction lay attraction, flirting, but nothing more. The integrity of his investigation would be untouched and he wouldn't have to worry about being neatly caught in a romantic speed trap.

If he took the other fork, if he let her into his confidence and his life, they'd cross a bridge right now. The Relationship Bridge. Was he ready to take that kind of step?

He thought about Julia in his arms last night, warm and pliant. He thought about her pixie grin, her tender but tough spirit, her slightly skewed perspective on the world. And he thought about the state of constant physical arousal he'd been living in lately.

Hell, yes, he was good and ready.

"Like *what?*" Julia repeated. She rose slowly until she stood a fraction of an inch away from him, holding his gaze. Her tongue glided across the edge of her upper lip.

A burning need filled him to trace the same path with his own. And—*oh, God.* She was watching his mouth. He caught his breath as he felt the reverberations deep inside his diaphragm.

He pulled his mind forcibly away from thoughts like that. Even his body edged backwards a bit as he shoved his hands in his pockets. Right now, he needed to talk more than he needed to kiss her.

He had a hell of a lot of explaining to do, didn't he? Explanations that could end up earning him an unpaid, unasked-for, maybe even permanent, vacation from the police department.

"You don't know a damned thing about me," he said roughly.

Her gaze faltered. After a moment, she said, "I know you're honorable."

"Honorable?"

"Uh-huh. And… and…" She stopped, blushing.

Rick gave her a sour grin. "Can't think of anything else nice to say?"

"No! It's not that, it's just, well, everything I

wanted to say would have made you sound like a Boy Scout or something. You know—kind, and brave, and honest —stuff like that."

"Kind, brave, honest? Honey, you've got the wrong guy."

"I must have forgotten to include *modest,* too." Julia smiled.

But the word she'd said first—*honorable*— kept pounding in the back of Rick's head.

At dawn, when he'd been thinking all this through, it had been easy to convince himself that he could juggle an investigation and a growing attraction to Julia. In the cold, hard light of day, he thought he must have been crazy.

He couldn't do it. He couldn't rationalize away the ethical issues. Every minute he spent here, technically he was on duty. And by virtue of accidental proximity, she was involved in the case he was investigating. There was no getting around it.

So... he couldn't go to bed with Julia unless he told her who he really was, and he couldn't tell her who he really was during the course of this investigation. How long? Days, weeks, months?

Damn it all.

"If that's what you're thinking, maybe we need to slow down here. I'm not your typical nice guy."

Julia's expression closed up instantly and she backed away a step. "Sorry, my mistake."

There was no misunderstanding the defensive sarcasm in her voice. Rick's insides twisted. He reached for her without thought. "Julia…"

She slipped out his grasp and moved toward the counter. "I'll make a fresh pot of coffee. This one's almost gone."

"Julia." He stepped in front of her.

She stopped, refusing to look at him. "Look, last night's still kind of hazy. I understand if you aren't interested in—"

"That's not it and you know it."

"I don't know a thing, as you so kindly pointed out. All I know is, I'm getting real tired of this conversation."

Her expression was stubbornly unconcerned, but the slump in her shoulders told Rick what he needed to know.

Okay, new scenario. What if he could balance the two sides? Let nature take its course, without blowing the investigation? It wouldn't go on forever. In fact, there should be some arrests made within the next few weeks, and by then he and Julia would probably be tired of each other anyway. No harm done. Right?

Rick grunted in agreement with himself and took a deep breath. "I didn't mean that the way it sounded. Would you just stand still for a minute and listen to me?"

"Maybe."

She flinched when he reached for her again. Cursing under his breath, he restricted himself to brushing her hair away from her face. Then his hands came to rest on her shoulders.

"If it sounded like I was saying last night was a mistake, that isn't what I meant. I'd like to see more of you. If you're interested. Okay?"

"Maybe. What about the fact that I don't know a damned thing about you? Are you planning on enlightening me any time soon? Or are you going to be mysterious about it?"

Rick looked away for a moment. "This is a... an unusual situation I'm in. I can't tell you more than that, so you'll have to trust me. Can you do that?"

"Do you by any chance know someone named Danny Spinelli?"

"Who?"

"Never mind. Just tell me, are you doing anything illegal?"

"No." He met her eye. At least that was one thing he could be honest about. "No. I'm operating strictly on the up and up. And in a couple of weeks, when everything's settled, I'll tell you all about it. Will you trust me till then?"

Julia closed her eyes for a few seconds and took a slow, deep breath. Then she looked at him. "Okay. I'll do it." She exhaled on a sigh. "I trust you."

"You do?"

She nodded, unsmiling. "Don't sound so surprised. I still think you're a pretty decent guy, even if you can't make up your mind about it." Her gaze shifted away from his. "I guess I'll be the last to know if I'm being stupid again, huh?"

"Again?" Rick didn't like the troubled look that had appeared on her face. "What's that supposed to mean?"

Her eyes shot back to him. "Nothing. Never mind." She backed away a step, not far enough to force his hands off her shoulders, but suddenly there was cool air between them instead of body heat. Her voice was so soft he had to strain to hear her words. "Let's just take this slowly, okay? See how it goes?"

"Yeah. Right." *Slowly, hell.* He slid his fingers around to cup the back of her neck and pulled her closer again. She didn't resist. His other hand slipped off her shoulder and down to her waist.

Now she moved in on her own, until her breasts grazed his chest. When she looked up, her mouth slightly open as if she was having trouble taking in enough air, he touched his lips to hers.

And exploded with unassuaged passion.

Hauling her up against him, he drove his tongue into her mouth. She opened for him, inviting deeper intimacy. Every cell in his being screamed for release. He wanted her here, now, standing up or lying on the kitchen floor, it didn't matter where. His fingers tightened in her hair as his other hand moved lower and cradled her fleece-clad bottom, hugging her close to his rocketing arousal. She moaned, heating him to a fever of desire that promised paradise if he could only survive a few more seconds of this unrelenting torture.

Suddenly Julia jerked away from him, breathing hard. Her cheeks glowed a deep rose. "Hold it... right... there." She backed away, clenching her fists.

Rick's head felt as empty as his arms. Pain blazed from his groin outward to the rest of his body. "What happened?"

"I thought we decided we were going to take it slow."

He swallowed the socially-unacceptable word that jumped to his lips. "You decided."

"We agreed."

"And that's supposed to mean hands-off? That isn't slow, it's nonexistent."

"I didn't mean hands-off, exactly. Just... I guess we ought to get to know each other better first. Yes, that's what I mean."

"You've gotta be kidding." Rick moved to the kitchen table and nearly fell into his chair... but very slowly, very carefully. "Let me get this straight. You say you trust me enough to, uh, pursue a relationship, but you don't know me well enough to let me touch you." He looked up at her. "Your scruples are showing up pretty damned late here."

His scowl didn't seem to faze Julia at all. She glared back at him. "You're deliberately misunderstanding me. That isn't what I meant at all. I just don't like to rush into something until I'm sure of what I'm doing."

"You could have fooled me," he muttered

under his breath, but she heard him anyway.

With a sigh, she slipped into the chair opposite his and leaned across the table, her expression solemn. "Never mind my behavior over the past few days. I'm *not* looking for a casual fling... I've never been good at those. Please, tell me now if that's all you want."

Rick felt the humor seeping back into him. "What's so terrible about a casual fling now and then?"

"Come on. I'm serious."

"What else is new?" But she had him treed for the moment. If he admitted that he wasn't likely to give her what she wanted, it would shoot every chance he had with her to hell and back. On the other hand, the thought of committing himself to something more than the most unstructured dealings with any woman had him twitching in his seat.

Or maybe he was twitching with unfulfilled lust. Rick re-thought his goals.

Maybe he could manage a few quiet nights at home. He grinned, wondering if Julia would snuggle up with him on the sofa while they watched reruns of *Hill Street Blues*. The idea sounded unexpectedly gratifying.

He should have been nervous, but he wasn't quite. It was kind of like skiing fast down a hill you knew was just a little too steep for your skills. It was scary but exhilarating.

"I guess... you could say... sure, we could

give it a try and see where it goes," he admitted half-grudgingly.

Her smile almost blinded him. The elusive dimple appeared and her eyes brightened. "I knew it! I knew you weren't as superficial as you always try to sound."

"Just remember I warned you. Maybe you're no good at casual stuff, but I've never been much good at anything but."

"Really and truly?" Her eyebrows rose. "You've never been serious about *anyone?*"

Rick's twitch returned. "No. Well, I was married once—" He stopped speaking. The floor had begun to vibrate as pounding came from somewhere in the building. He heard Shemp woof-woofing next door. In the other room, Poppy growled and then gave one high-pitched bark—before settling back down to sleep, no doubt.

"Is that your front door?"

"No, I'm sure it isn't." Julia shook her head impatiently. "Now what were you just saying about—"

A voice from outside floated into the room. It sounded like Bigelow. "Hey, you! You in there? I gotta talk to you." The pounding resumed.

"It's *my* door."

"Yes, but what about—"

Rick rose quickly, almost knocking over his chair. "I have to run. Sorry. Catch you later."

He strode out of the kitchen before Julia had a chance to say another word. She sat at the table,

stunned, as the front door slammed shut behind
him. After a second or two, she hopped out of her
chair and followed. But her hand slowed and
came to rest on the door knob as she strained to
hear the male voices on the porch.

"... and it better be good." That was Rick,
irritated and blustering. Julia smiled in spite of
herself.

"I figured you'd want to know that what's-his-
name in B-3 was lookin' for you. How-*ever,* if
you're too busy to be interrupted at the moment—"

"Mind your own damn business, Bigelow."

Julia could almost see the smirk being wiped
from the apartment manager's face. He'd always
given her the creeps, and she had to admit to taking
a certain amount of pleasure in Rick's giving him
his comeuppance. But what kind of a way was that
for an employee to speak to a supervisor? How
could Rick expect to get away with it?

"Well, if that's the way you feel, then you
prob'ly don't want to know what I heard Williams
tell that big dumb flunky of his, right?"

After a brief pause, she heard Rick's voice
again. "Inside, Bigelow. We can talk inside my
place."

There was a shuffle of footsteps, and Rick's
front door opened and closed. His dog barked one
more time. "Settle down, Shemp. It's just me."

Their voices faded as the men moved from
the entryway farther into the townhouse.
Disappointed, Julia went back to the kitchen and

picked up her coffee mug. It was still half full, but what was left was cold. Making another pot now seemed like more trouble than it was worth.

"Oh, the heck with it." Instead, she washed the rest of the dishes. Thoughts of Rick swarmed through her head.

I was married once...

Just like that? It had been a throwaway line, after he'd said he'd never had a serious relationship. He didn't seem to take anything seriously—not even a marriage.

What's-his-name in B-3 was lookin' for you...

That must be the infamous Mr. Williams, supposedly an ex-convict. And Rick was hanging around with him. Not a good sign at all. She'd had her fill of men who walked the edge of the law, sometimes toppling to the wrong side.

Julia pushed her hair back with sudsy fingers. No, she wasn't going to do this to herself. Danny Spinelli had been on her mind too much lately, that was all. She was expecting Rick to turn out as bad as Danny. But comparing the two was like comparing apples and oranges.

Let's face it. Terry was right. You've been looking for reasons not to trust him, just like you always do.

She squared her shoulders and attacked the dishes with renewed vigor. It was time she stopped living in the past and shying away from men out of simple insecurity.

Chapter Seven

❖   ❖   ❖

Who the hell was Danny Spinelli?

It was driving Rick crazy. Who was the guy and what was he to Julia? If she thought he hadn't been paying attention when she'd said the name, she was dead wrong. After all, he'd been trained to notice every minor detail.

He couldn't even concentrate on the regular Monday morning squad meeting. The six members of his vice team sat in borrowed chairs, crowded around the old steel desk in his fifth-floor office at the Hall of Justice. While they gave progress reports on their current cases, all Rick could think about was Julia. What she'd said. How she'd looked and felt and smelled.

All day Sunday he'd been across the bridge in Berkeley, helping his brother-in-law build a red-wood deck in the backyard. When he'd returned to the townhouse after dinner, Julia's apartment had been dark. Had she been out with a man? Danny Spinelli, maybe?

Not that he was worried about it, of course.

Rick shook his head to clear it. He was supposed to be running this meeting, not daydreaming about some female. And it was his turn to report on the status of his cases.

"Well, I think everyone knows what's going on with Williams. I moved into the place—"

"My back remembers that," D.J. said. "I can't believe the city was too cheap to pay for rental furniture and we had to move your two-ton sofa."

Rick gave him a grin. "Hey, life is hard. Anyway, I made contact, and put in a lot of time at Shelby's, which is Darryl Williams's favorite known hangout and usual place of business." He raised his hands, palm side up. "All that's left is to continue to be available, and hold out for a big cocaine buy. I think it's working. Williams sold me an eight-ball… an eighth of a kilo… the other day."

A round of spotty applause greeted his announcement.

"But it isn't enough yet," he went on. "I want to put this guy away for a *long* time. I'm holding out for four or five kilos. That ought to do it."

"Good luck, Rick," said Penny O'Malley, the only woman in his unit of the Vice Control Division. "You're gonna need it with Darryl Williams. He's unpredictable."

Next, Steel reported on his ongoing investigation of a suspected bookmaking operation. "Bennington's real slick. I'm not going to get anything on him unless I can get in there and dig a little deeper. How about an undercover gig?"

Rick shrugged. "Maybe when the Williams case is wrapped up. I can't spare you right now. But I'll run it by the lieutenant when I talk to him."

"What did the looey say about your idea for an organized crime task force? Then I could really concentrate on the Bennington case. If you take me with you, that is."

"Stay in line and I'll think about it." Rick leaned back in his chair with a satisfied smile. "Looey's pitching the idea to the brass. Captain Mitchell likes it, so maybe it'll fly eventually. But you know how slowly things happen around here."

The other guys had been sitting around half-listening, but now Arthur Franklin gave a dry laugh. "You'll have your lieutenant's bars and be long gone by then."

"Yeah, sarge," said Penny. "But no rush. We'll probably get stuck with Artie in charge and then where'll we be?" With a snicker, she ducked to avoid a paper airplane sent her way by Arthur.

"Meeting's adjourned, boys and girls. Go play outside. Steel, I need to talk to you before you head out."

After the others wandered off, Steel said, "What's up?"

"I want you to be available by pager and cellular phone if I need you, okay? We may have to rush the buy if Williams will go for it. The lieutenant's been breathing down my neck about making this quick and clean."

Any round-the-clock undercover operation was too expensive and too dangerous to justify continuing long without an arrest. The apartment complex management had popped for his cover and the use of the townhouse; the owners were just as eager to get rid of Williams as Rick was. But as D.J. had complained, he'd had to bring the bare necessities of life from his own place.

He needed to wrap this up before it all fell apart on one side or the other. Most of all, he needed to resolve the thing with Julia before he totally lost his mind.

Wondering again where she'd been the previous night, he muttered aloud, "Danny *Spinelli.*"

"Danny Spinelli?" echoed Steel. "Is he in town again? Jeez, I thought we'd seen the last of him."

"What?" Rick looked up, too surprised to hide his interest. "What do you know about Danny Spinelli?"

"I arrested him."

"What? When? What for?"

Steel gave him a funny look. "Years ago, when I was a rookie beat cop. For armed robbery and… let me see, possession of stolen property. Why? Is he involved with Williams now?"

"No… no." Rick flushed. "I just heard his name somewhere. Tell me about it."

"There's nothing much to tell," Steel said with a shrug. "But I did run into Danny again a few years ago, after he got out of prison. He told me he was moving to New Jersey. Had some relatives there, I guess. He seemed subdued. Prison does that to some guys."

"What about the armed robbery?"

"What about it? He held up a convenience store in the Mission. Seems to me they set off a silent alarm. Anyway, we got him pulling out of the parking lot. Like I said, not much to it. So what's going on? Is he back in town again or what?"

It was almost uncanny, the way cops remembered so many names and faces, so many arrests. But Steel wouldn't know anything more; a detective would have taken over investigating the case after the arrest had been made. "I don't think so. I was just curious about him. No big deal."

"Yeah, right." Steel was watching him, and Rick could tell the moment realization dawned in his eyes. "So that's it—I remember now. It's *her,* isn't it? She was Spinelli's girlfriend."

Rick mumbled something unintelligible.

"Don't worry," Steel said pragmatically. "I doubt she recognized me. I only saw her the one time in court, and that was, oh, seven years ago, I guess. Besides, she probably didn't even notice me there. Too caught up in her own problems."

"What do you mean?"

"She didn't tell you? Her testimony helped put him away. It always stuck in my mind, how scared she seemed on the stand. She was only about nineteen or twenty at the time. It took a lot of guts to get up there and testify against her lover like that."

Rick sat in his office after Steel left, staring blindly at the news clippings and mug shots that decorated his office walls. Finally he got up and made a trip down to the fourth floor and the Records Division.

Half an hour later he was back at his desk, the office door closed as he paged through the fading documents in Danny Spinelli's case file. The investigating officer had conducted a thorough interview with Julia almost eight years ago. The standard form gave her name, address, age. Rick buzzed through them. She hadn't lived in the cozy Noe Valley townhouse in those days; instead, a low-rent street in the Mission District had been her home base. He flipped back a few pages. Spinelli had given the same address.

Occupation: waitress/student. She'd been working her way through college when she'd managed to almost wreck her life by hooking up with pond scum like Danny. Rick shook his head. Some kids seemed irrationally bent on screwing up. He'd had to learn the hard way himself, hadn't he?

The gist of Julia's statement was that, without her knowledge, Danny Spinelli had been using her home to store stolen property from residential burglaries. That was before he branched out into armed robberies, for which he used Julia's car. Basically, he'd been doing a pretty good job of just plain using *Julia*. Once he was arrested and she discovered what had been going on, she cooperated fully with the police investigation.

Rick's cynical heart softened a bit at the thought of Julia caught up in the criminal justice system.

It had been touch-and-go there for a while. She'd been considered an accessory at the time this statement was taken. Once the detective had actually talked to her, though, he'd pitched that idea. It was obvious that Julia's innate honesty had shone through just as clearly at nineteen as it did now.

And it was no wonder that she clung to her respectability like a lifeline these days, either.

Julia was exhausted by the time she arrived home from school on Monday. She hadn't gotten much rest Friday night, of course, and then she'd been too tense to sleep well on Saturday. Last night she'd gone to the movies with some of her teacher friends. It was a high-flown, intellectual—and unfortunately, slow-moving—kind of film, and she'd almost faded out midway through. She'd managed to stay awake, but it had been a late night for a Sunday, and now she was ready to drop.

Until Rick appeared at the door, of course.

"I'm taking Shemp out for a run at Golden Gate Park." He cocked a heavy brow at her. "Are your feet okay? Wanna come along?"

He was a vision in a tropical-print shirt, sweat

pants and a fanny pack. Despite her misgivings, Julia couldn't help the bolt of gratification that shot through her. "How could I refuse such a gracious invitation?"

He grinned, and her misgivings tumbled away. "Hey, it worked, didn't it?"

"Let me change and get Poppy's leash. We'll be right out."

"A leash?" he called after her. "What kind of a weenie are you, anyway?"

"A law-abiding one," she muttered under her breath. She and the properly-restrained Poppy joined him outside a few minutes later. It was all she could do to keep a straight face when he waved to Mrs. McCully, standing watch at her kitchen window.

They reached the garage and Julia took a look at Rick's sports car. "No way are we all going to fit into that thing."

"It'll be fine. I'll drive, and Shemp and Poppy can sit in your lap."

"Not a chance."

"Okay, Shemp can drive and you can sit in my lap."

She shot him a teacher look, then spoiled the effect by smiling. "How about we take my car, and the dogs sit in the back?"

"You've got a deal."

While she unlocked the passenger door, he reached into his car and came up with a long strip of woven blue nylon. Julia heaved a long-suffering sigh. "Are my eyes deceiving me, or is that object a leash?"

"I hope you don't think I'd consider breaking the park rules," Rick said, his tone as prim as a maiden aunt's.

"It never crossed my mind." *Hmmph. Weenie, indeed.*

Trying to move around to the other side of the car without tripping over the dogs, she bumped into him. He reached out to steady her, grasping her upper arms, and her breath caught. His hands were warm and strong. She hadn't felt them on her body in two long days. It unnerved her to realize how quickly she'd learned to covet his touch. Resisting the urge to step closer, she glanced up at his face. He was watching her in a way that made her fingertips tingle.

Then Poppy snarled at Shemp, and the intimacy vanished. Julia looked away, still unsure of how she felt about him or about the two of them. He hadn't released her arms yet. With a smile directed at his collarbone, she said, "I don't know who's worse, you or those dogs. You're both always underfoot."

"Maybe it's you, not being careful where you step."

"I do try to watch where I'm going."

One side of his mouth quirked upwards. "Yeah, that's what I figured."

Somehow the conversation had taken a turn for the symbolic. Well, he wasn't going to trap her into saying something she didn't mean. Her smile spread and turned genuine. "It's better than walking straight into, um, deep doo-doo."

Rick laughed and patted her cheek. "Smart lady." He turned away, opening the back door so the dogs could hop into the car, then folded himself into the passenger seat.

Julia drove across town at her usual sedate pace. Rick fidgeted. "Do you want me to drive?"

She gave him a sideways look. "I think not."

"It could be tomorrow before we get there, you know."

"That's okay. The park isn't going anywhere without us."

Golden Gate Park was the heart of the city, and a popular recreation area. At this hour on a weekday, though, it wasn't horribly crowded. Julia managed to park not too far from the redwood and eucalyptus-lined walking trails.

They untangled the leashes and let the dogs out of the car. Poppy was wild with excitement, yanking on her leash and trying to pull Julia along. Shemp, older and evidently more accustomed to the scenery, followed at a slower pace with Rick in tow.

A few yards off the main trail, any sign of civilization disappeared. No one else was around. Julia realized that spring finally seemed to be moving in; the trees were greener today. The air seemed fresher and clearer, the flowers more profuse, the paths more interesting than she'd ever noticed before.

Or maybe having Rick by her side just made it seem that way. She shook her head, unsettled but happy to be there.

Rick cleared his throat. "So. This is a great place to bring the dogs."

"It sure is. I don't know why Poppy and I don't do this much. I usually just walk her in the neighborhood."

"You grew up in the city. You must have spent a lot of time here when you were a kid."

She shook her head. "Not really. These days I get here more often. I like to go to the museums and the Japanese tea garden, stuff like that. I just don't usually bring my dog. But maybe I will, now that you've reminded me how much fun it is."

"So what *did* you do for fun back then?"

"Back when?"

"When you were a kid." Impatience threaded through his voice.

Julia kicked at a rock on the path. "Oh, you know. The usual stuff kids do. What about you? Did you hang around here much? There's lots of neat things for kids... the aquarium, the playground, all that stuff."

"I know. We made it over here once in a while on a Sunday afternoon. But I grew up in—in the Eastbay, don't forget." He shifted Shemp's leash to the other side and reached over to take her hand, lacing their fingers together. The heat that always seemed to simmer between them flared instantly. "Are you a member of a secret organization or something?"

She flushed. "What do you mean?"

"You know exactly what I mean. Every time I ask you a personal question, you change the subject."

"That's not true." *Yes, it is, you coward.* "There's just nothing interesting to say. My life is so normal it's boring."

"Sure. Tell me about your parents."

"They're gone."

"Tell me something I don't already know."

She took a deep breath. "My mother died when I was nineteen."

"What about your dad?"

"Look, why don't you tell me about *your* parents?"

She started to pull her hand away, but he tightened his grip and stopped walking, forcing her and the dogs to stop, too. She turned to meet his gaze.

"Don't push me." His voice had gone cold, his expression hard.

He wasn't the only one who could get mad. "Don't threaten *me*." She yanked her hand out of his and started walking again. Poppy had to scramble to keep up with her this time.

Rick caught up quickly. "Okay. I'm sorry. It's just so damned frustrating sometimes."

"What is?" Julia kept her eyes focused straight ahead.

"Trying to talk to you."

"Go ahead. Talk your heart out."

"Maybe I will."

The path curved around a clump of trees and then widened. Rick plunked himself down on a big stump sitting off to the side and called Shemp over.

"What are you doing?"

"Taking off his leash. I want to let him run for awhile."

"But—"

"I know. It's against the park rules. But we're miles away from anyone else here. It won't be a problem. I promise."

"Mmph."

"Quit sulking and come sit down with me."

"I don't sulk," Julia said indignantly.

He grinned up at her. "You've gotta be kidding."

She narrowed her eyes at him. He laughed, and she ended up smiling. As she settled onto the stump, one last disapproving thought occurred to her. "I'll probably end up getting splinters, sitting on this thing."

"Don't worry. I'll pick them out with tweezers and a magnifying glass. Every last one of them, slowly and carefully. And I'll take great pleasure in the job."

It sounded so ridiculous that she laughed. Then she thought about it again and it sounded less ridiculous, more sensuous. Sensuous enough to send a shiver through her.

"Stop squirming. You're probably picking up more slivers."

She sat still. But the vision of him running his hands over her bare bottom, slowly and carefully, wouldn't go away. Sitting still had never been more difficult.

Rick reached into his fanny pack and pulled out a tennis ball, then threw it far down the path. Shemp took off. Poppy whined and pulled on her leash.

"Don't you want to let her take off for a while, too?"

"She'll get lost."

"No, she won't. She'll stick close by Shemp."

"Uh-uh."

"Okay." He took out a smaller rubber ball and rolled it toward Poppy. She dove after it, then trotted over to drop it at his feet. They repeated the process a couple of times, with Rick taking a break to throw the drippy tennis ball for Shemp, too.

Finally Julia said, "*What* is she doing?"

"Retrieving."

"Dachshunds don't retrieve."

"This one does. Shemp and I taught her. You'd better put some of these in her Easter basket."

Julia pictured an Easter basket full of doggy treats, flea spray and little rubber balls, and she dissolved into laughter.

"Hey, it wasn't that funny."

"I know. It's just... I..." She lost it again. Rick

watched her, looking amused and indulgent. When she'd calmed down, she said, "Don't mind me. I seem to be going through a difficult stage at the moment." One more tiny hiccup of laughter escaped.

"Second childhood?"

"Maybe so." She stopped, hoping he didn't intend to pursue the subject of her childhood yet again.

Instead, he surprised her. "I bet you'd like my sister. She'd probably understand whatever the hell it is you're laughing about. You two could giggle together while everyone else sat around looking confused."

"You have a sister?"

"Yep. A brother, too. He's older, she's younger. I'm a classic middle child."

Why was she always surprised to think of him as part of a family, part of society? Maybe it was because there was so much about him that she didn't know. At any rate, she was dying to hear more about his life.

Poppy brought Rick her ball again and yipped impatiently when he didn't reach for it right away. Julia gave up. "I guess I might as well let her run, too."

She leaned over to unfasten the leash. Rick tossed the ball far into the trees, and Poppy took off so fast that Julia could hardly see her little legs moving. She straightened and turned back to Rick. "I was an only child. Tell me what it was like growing up with siblings."

He shrugged. "It was okay. They were just *there,* bent on making my life miserable. These days, I guess I like having them around. We're pretty close."

"Do they live around here?"

"Mary Ann's in Berkeley. Sam lives in San Diego and doesn't get up this way much any more. But we talk sometimes."

"That's nice. I always wanted a sister or brother. What about your parents? Where are they?"

"Out of the country."

Julia laughed. "No, I meant, where do they live?"

"Oh. They still live in the house we grew up in."

"Where was that?"

He mumbled something she couldn't quite understand.

"Where?"

His face was turning red. "I said, Piedmont."

"Piedmont?" Julia sat in stunned silence for a moment. "You grew up in *Piedmont?*"

He nodded, looking sheepish.

It was one of the most elegant, exclusive communities in the entire Bay Area. Now she had a big job ahead of her, reconciling her concept of Rick with a totally different picture suggested by the fact that he'd grown up in Piedmont, of all places. "You're rich!"

One corner of his mouth quirked up. "Not me. My folks maybe, but I'm definitely working class."

"I guess so." Julia blinked, still trying to put it together. What had happened since the Piedmont upbringing to put him where he was today? "What do your parents do?"

Rick shook his head. "I brought this on myself, didn't I? My dad's an attorney. He's the senior partner in a firm in the Financial District. Mom is... well, she used to be sort of a society type, but she's given it up for a life of adventure lately. She drags my father off on these weird trips all the time."

"Oh."

"She's even starting to think about it as a career, planning adventure trips for groups of older people. Those years of running fundraisers for the hospital guild are paying off, I guess. And all that time we thought charity balls were for fluffheads."

His parents sounded different from anyone Julia had ever met in her life. Actually, her life was beginning to seem pretty circumscribed compared to Rick's. Where did he fit into that picture of wealthy people and their lives of luxury?

She'd already asked so many nosy questions. But if he was in the mood to talk... She took a deep breath. "What about your wife?"

"My what?"

"You told me you'd been married."

"Yeah. It was a long time ago. Come on, let's go. We can talk about it while we look for the dogs."

"The dogs?" Julia jumped up, startled. She'd forgotten all about them. Now she realized that she hadn't seen or heard either of them in ages. The sun was getting low in the sky, and she started to panic. "I *told* you that wretched little mutt would run off and get lost."

"She'll show up." Rick pursed his lips and gave a long, high-pitched whistle. Then he headed down the path. "Come on."

Julia followed, calling, "Poppy! Come on, time to go home. Poppy! It's dinner time, baby."

After a minute, Shemp ambled down the trail in their direction. Rick hooked up his leash. But there was no sign of her dog. Julia's dread grew. "*Poppy!* Where are you?"

"Don't worry, she'll come when she's good and ready. They always do."

Just as Rick finished speaking, Shemp growled. A second later came the familiar sound of Poppy barking wildly. There was a rustle in the shrubbery and then a squirrel scampered up a tree.

"Poppy?" Rick said, his voice deep and authoritative. "Get out here and leave that squirrel alone. Or you won't be invited back."

Poppy trotted obediently out of the bushes and rolled onto her back, seeking approval from Rick. Julia was disgusted. "I can't believe you ignore me, and then jump to do his bidding. You little traitor." She grabbed Poppy's collar and attached the leash before the dog could take off again.

Rick held out a hand. "I'll take her, if you want."

"Okay. I think she likes you better than me, anyway."

When Julia stood up and gave him the leash, he transferred both to the other hand and reached out again. This time he wrapped an arm around her waist and pulled her against him. Before she could even register any surprise, his mouth came down on hers. The kiss was long and slow and sweet, and she lost all sense of herself before he ended it and raised his head. Then she discovered her arms were hugging his mid-section. And she found she didn't really want to let go, either.

Rick looked down at her, still in the shelter of his arms, and he grinned. "Sorry. You looked so put out, I just couldn't help myself."

"It wasn't so bad."

"It was damn good, and you know it."

"Okay," she agreed. "It *was* damn good."

His smile spread and grew smug. He nuzzled her temple, his breath warm against her ear. She loved the soft brush of his beard on her cheek, the weight of his hands at the waistband of her jeans. It wasn't one of those *I-want-your-body* embraces. Of course, that kind was pretty wonderful, too. But this one was a comfort to her soul.

Just as she was thinking she could stand there with him forever, he pulled away. "Come on, we'd better go. It's starting to get dark."

Julia nearly had to run to keep up with Rick

and the dogs. She was already breathless when, halfway back to civilization, he slowed down and said casually, "About my marriage."

"Oh, so you weren't trying to change the subject back there, after all?"

"Do you want to hear this or not?"

"Only if you want to talk about it." It came out sounding so prissy that she was embarrassed. "I mean, go ahead."

"There wasn't much to it. We were in college, and we thought we knew what we were doing. But it was a mistake from start to finish. Four years of... well, not hell exactly, but close enough. We should have gotten out after four months."

He probably wasn't even aware of how bitter he sounded. Julia told herself not to ask. Even so, the soft words slipped out. "What happened?"

He stared ahead blindly and didn't answer right away. Then he shrugged. "Typical story. We were young and dumb. Neither of us was very careful, and she turned up pregnant. We got married in a hurry. A month later she miscarried. We tried to make a go of it, but eventually the whole thing fell apart."

Julia couldn't contain the smile flowering on her face. "But you did the right thing. There are so many men who don't accept their responsibilities."

It was a mild speech that hardly began to express what she felt. Flashing lights, confetti and fireworks went off inside her head. Her stomach did jumping-jacks and her heart danced.

All because Rick had married his pregnant girlfriend over a decade ago. All because he really was turning out to be the kind of man a woman could respect and trust.

And love. Yes, definitely. She could love a man like that.

By the time they got home, it was full dark. Julia heard Rick swear and she looked over to find him staring at his watch. He hopped out of the car almost before it stopped moving and hauled Shemp back to his apartment.

Before he left again, he managed a fast goodbye kiss for her as she stood on the porch fiddling with her keys. "I gotta head out. Sorry."

"Oh? Where are you off to now?" she said sweetly.

"I just have to, uh, go somewhere. But I meant to fix that kitchen light for you. I didn't get to it yesterday."

"It's all taken care of—I replaced the wire nuts and put up the new cover. And it's working fine now."

Rick laughed. "*You* did it all by yourself? I'm impressed."

"Very funny, Mr. Handyman. I looked up how in a book. And at least the cover will stay up this time."

"Yeah, go ahead and zap me when I'm already

in disgrace." He gave her a grin and ran down the steps, waving as he left.

"Well, it was fun while it lasted," Julia told Poppy. "Come on, let's go inside. It's time for dinner."

The message light on her answering machine was blinking when she went in. She pushed the play button, and the messages rewound while she opened a can of dog food.

Actually, she had some trouble with the can opener. Excitement and elation filled her, and her fingers shook. She knew she was on the brink of a momentous experience, and for once in her life, she intended to fling herself into it headlong instead of backing safely away from the edge.

The first message on the machine was from Terry. "Hi, Jules. Just wanted to let you know, I talked to my cousin Paul. He's going to check out this Rick Perry guy and get back to me. I'll call again when I hear something more. Meanwhile, behave yourself."

"Oh, Lord." Julia's face flamed. What if Rick had been here with her when she'd played back that message? She was going to kill Terry... if she didn't have a stroke first. She thought she felt one coming on.

The tape beeped and the next message played. "Hi, Ms. Newman, it's me, Kathleen. I just wanted to say hi, 'cause I'm not scared or anything. But you can call me back if you want."

Julia smiled. Kathleen had called and talked to

the answering machine for fifteen minutes that first night, when she'd had been out. She'd called every night since then, too, but each call and message had been shorter than the last. She'd seemed happy in school today. Overall, she appeared to be adjusting well to her mother's job and her own new-found independence.

Maybe, Julia thought, she'd wait a bit to return the call. Then she might catch Kathleen's mother at home and see what she had to say about the situation.

After a quick dinner, she checked over her lesson plans for the rest of the week. Spring break was coming up, and she wanted to cram in what she could before the kids started going wild in anticipation.

At nine o'clock, she picked up the phone and dialed Kathleen's number. A woman answered. Julia launched into her spiel. "Hello, Mrs. Simmons? This is Julia Newman, Kathleen's teacher."

"Miss Newman? From school? Oh, Miss Newman, thank you for what you done for my baby."

"I've just been trying to help her adjust to her new routine. She does seem more settled now."

"You made her so happy, she's like a new little person. And I was so worried about her before. You're a miracle worker, Miss Newman."

Warmth spread through Julia. This had to be one of the nicest days of her life. "Kathleen's the one who deserves all the credit. You should be very proud of her. Now, I wanted to talk to you about your work schedule and Kathleen's care."

There was silence on the other end of the line. Then Mrs. Simmons said, "She goes to after-school care. The city pays for it. But there's no one to watch her at night. I don't make enough to pay for it yet."

Julia sighed silently. This was the point at which, if she suspected neglect, she was supposed to inform the woman that she *had* to work it out, or face a child welfare investigation.

She couldn't do it. Not to a woman who was so obviously concerned about the child's welfare herself. Not when she was doing everything she could to provide for the child. Nothing in that picture suggested neglect.

"Tell me, Mrs. Simmons, how long does Kathleen have to stay alone each night?"

"My neighbor picks her up at six o'clock and brings her here. Then I get home by eight-thirty."

"What about Saturday and Sunday? Does she stay by herself all day?"

"Oh no, Miss Newman. I don't work on the weekends, only Monday through Friday. I'm home with my baby on the weekends."

"But—" Julia stopped short. So what if Kathleen had called both nights over the weekend? If it made her feel more secure, it was fine.

"My boss says, if I do good, I can have a day shift in a few weeks. Then I'd always be home

with Kathleen. I'm doin' real good, Miss Newman,
I really am. I don't want to lose this job."

"No, of course not. And if you can work during
the day instead, that's even better. I'll keep an eye
on Kathleen at school, though. If she can't handle
the responsibility, something will have to be done."

"I understand, I do."

"And keep me posted about your work schedule,
okay? So I know what's going on with her."

"Yes, ma'am."

Julia hung up the phone with a chuckle. There
was nothing on earth more guaranteed to make
her feel like a teacher than hearing "yes, ma'am."
Still, in today's world, it wasn't something she
heard often.

Kathleen's problems seemed to be working
themselves out, thank goodness. Julia wasn't
surprised. It had been an absolutely matchless day
for problems to work themselves out.

Chapter Eight

❖   ❖   ❖

Rick spent most of Thursday sitting in Shelby's with Darryl Williams. By the end of the day, he felt sure the guy trusted him. Now all he had to do was wait. When Williams was ready, the big buy would happen, and Rick would have him cold.

He pulled the Porsche into the garage he shared with Julia. Before he'd even opened the car door, she pulled in next to him. It was downright embarrassing how his pulse rate speeded up when he saw her. But he was leaning against the Porsche, waiting, when she eased out of her car carrying a pile of clothing in cleaner's bags over one arm.

She shot him an annoyed look. "Men... cars... hmmph!"

He crossed his arms on the roof of the Honda and grinned across at her. "Having a bad day?"

"Of course not," Julia said airily. "But what did you say your name was?"

The question set Rick on edge for a moment

before he realized she meant it rhetorically, not seriously. Then he gave her his best smirk. "Did you miss me?"

"Not a chance." The princess look was back full-force.

So she'd noticed. For the past few days, he'd been avoiding her. She wrecked his concentration, and when he wasn't with her, he remembered all the reasons—personal and professional—why he ought to stay away.

Of course, it hadn't made much difference. Even when she wasn't around, she still wrecked his concentration. Wondering what was going on in her head, how she'd gotten hooked up with a small-time criminal, why she wouldn't talk about her past, still drove him crazy. But now he had a plan for finding out. Maybe if she weren't such a mystery woman, he wouldn't find her so damned enthralling.

"Hey, you're breaking my heart," he said, and she narrowed her eyes at him. "No, really. I've been so busy that I haven't been around much. But—"

"Busy doing what?"

"Oh, different stuff. But I was just on my way to see if you were home, anyway. Do you like Mexican food?"

"Who doesn't?" Her tone was still snippy, but one corner of her mouth lifted into a half-smile. And she didn't show any sign of marching out of the garage right this second.

"I know a great place for it out in the Mission."

"Uh-huh?"

"I thought you might like to have dinner tonight."

"Actually, that sounds wonderful. You wouldn't believe the time I've had." Her smile faded. "We don't have to go in my car again, do we?"

"No. Why? What's wrong with your car?"

She shrugged. "The stupid thing stalled right in the middle of 24th Street and I couldn't get it started again at first. It was so frustrating!"

"Oh yeah?" He glanced toward the hood and thought for a second. "Why don't we take your car after all, and see if it happens again. If I can figure out what's wrong, I can work on it this weekend."

"You don't need to do that."

"Haven't got anything better to do." Actually, he could think of a number of better things to do, but they all involved getting her naked. He'd be wise to stick with fixing the car.

❖   ❖   ❖

Following Rick's directions, Julia drove to the Taqueria Morales. The car didn't stall on the way. *It figures,* she thought. Whatever the problem, it seemed to have solved itself.

Guerrero Street was lined with small businesses and tumble-down shops, but the side streets were residential. They were getting close to the area in which she'd grown up. In fact, Solano Street, where she'd lived with her mother, was just ahead a few blocks. A drop of cold sweat trickled down her temple. She hadn't been back to this particular neighborhood in years.

She shouldn't have been the least bit surprised when Rick said, "Turn left here on Solano. There's usually some place to park a little way up the street."

Oh, Lord. A little way up the street, and they'd be right in front of Julia's old house. She didn't want to see it, no way, no how, not at all. There wasn't any point in dredging up unpleasant memories.

And since when have you been such a coward? She raised her chin and silently dared Solano Street to intimidate her.

The trouble was, after all these years, it still did.

As soon as they turned the corner, Rick said, "Look, there's a car coming out. You might as well grab the spot."

Saved by the battered Chevy pulling away from the curb. Julia felt calmer as she maneuvered into the empty space. She climbed out and slammed the door. Rick faced her over the roof of the car. "Are you all right? You look pale."

"Probably just stood up too fast."

"Probably. Well, don't forget to lock up."

"I lock the door automatically whenever I get out. I don't even have to think about it." Still, she checked all four doors with grim determination, then joined him on the sidewalk.

Strolling toward the intersection, Rick eyed two men squatting against the building at the end of the block and clasped Julia's hand loosely in his. His fingers tangled with hers and she realized he was being protective, not consciously perhaps, but warmth radiated through her anyway.

Funny how threatening these streets had seemed when she was a kid. Now it looked like any other rundown city neighborhood, seedy but not particularly frightening. When they turned the corner, she counted the businesses that remained from her childhood, along with the new additions. The liquor store was still there. Of course, it was probably the most profitable business on the block.

And there was Rosie's, the dusty old thrift shop where most of Julia's clothes had come from when she was small. She wondered if ancient, cranky Rosie still ran the store from her perch on a high stool behind the counter.

Dr. Castle, Painless Dentist, seemed to have closed down shop during Julia's seven-year absence. And there was an auto-parts store where—

"Here we go."

The Taqueria was housed in a large storefront that Julia barely recognized. She stopped and stared as Rick reached for the door. "Oh no, the dime store's gone."

"What dime store?"

She hadn't meant to say anything; it had just slipped out. Now she was stuck. "Right here where the restaurant is. In the old days it was a five-and-dime." Heavy dark-red curtains now covered the windows that used to display toys, kitchenwares and cheap clothing.

"The old days?"

Julia took a deep breath. She was making too big a deal about this. And Rick was no longer someone she could just brush off. Striving to keep her voice casual, she said, "I used to shop there when I was a kid. We lived around the corner."

"Oh yeah?" he said just as casually. But the way he watched her made her think of a large predator stalking its prey. "You'll have to show me the house."

"I will?"

"Come on, this door is heavy."

She skittered inside. The restaurant was dark, with ads for Mexican beer tacked up on the walls and the tingly fragrance of cilantro and chiles in the air. It was early and there weren't many customers yet. Rick chose a table for two near the back. It was so small that their knees knocked together underneath as they sat down.

"Ricardo! *Mijo!*"

Rick muttered something under his breath. Julia looked up.

A rotund, gray-haired man wearing a white apron grinned and waved to them from behind the counter in the back. Then he turned and yelled over his shoulder, "Hortensia! Get out here!"

Rick pushed back his chair and stood up. "Wait here," he told Julia as he took off toward the kitchen.

"Why?"

He stopped and frowned at her. "Because I need to talk to Luis about our dinner, okay?"

"Fine. Whatever."

A harried-looking woman bustled out of the kitchen, slapping a towel over her shoulder as she went. "What is it? Ah, Ricardo! We've missed you, *mijo.*"

Julia could only see Rick's back, but she heard the smile in his voice. "I won't stay away so long next time, Hope. Just haven't been around the neighborhood much lately, that's all."

He rested his hands on the counter and spoke to them in a low voice. The older couple leaned close to hear him. Their replies were just as quiet. Julia didn't stand a chance of catching a single word from this distance. At one point in the discussion, Hortensia—Hope—looked up at her and away again quickly. She and Luis nodded at Rick, and he returned to the table with the couple in tow.

Her face wreathed in smiles, Hortensia turned to Julia, who smiled back. They seemed like nice enough people and obviously they adored Rick. Even if he *was* the type who sneaked around and wouldn't let her hear his conversations. Hmmph!

"Welcome to the Taqueria..." The woman's

voice faded out and she looked uncertain. "Chulia?"

"Excuse me?"

"Chulia Newman, from Solano Street, yes?"

"I did live there years ago."

"You don't remember us, *mija?*"

Luis had a blank look on his face, and Hortensia elbowed him in his ample stomach. "Carole Newman's girl. A *nice* girl," she added as his eyes widened.

Baffled, Julia squinted at the couple. Then it hit her.

Carmel's parents!

She could see it all... the small white house bursting with life, a few doors away from her own empty home. As a kid she'd been too shy to mingle much, but she'd still been envious of her friend Carmel's big family and loving parents.

Eventually they'd moved to a larger house a few blocks away, Carmel had gone to a Catholic high school, and the girls had drifted apart. Julia hadn't seen the parents in at least twelve years. But she really ought to have recognized them right away.

She smiled, some of her youthful diffidence returning. "Mr. and Mrs. Morales. Yes, of course I remember you."

Rick was staring at her in undisguised shock. She sent him a bland smile.

"We heard about your mother, *pobrecita*. We were so sorry. You should have come to us."

"Thank you. It's nice to know someone cared."

"Where you been all these years?" asked Luis.
"Haven't seen you since... hey, I don't know
when."

Rick looked fascinated, Julia noticed. Her
hands twisted together in her lap, but she managed a smile for the Moraleses. "I still live here in
the city. How's your family? What are your kids
doing?"

It was a question calculated to turn the conversation away from herself, and it worked.
Hortensia gave her an overview of her children's
various accomplishments. When she stopped for a
breather, Rick winked at Julia and said, "You had
to ask."

Hortensia swatted the top of his head. "Wicked
boy!"

Julia had trouble meeting his gaze. He joked
around with the Moraleses, but there was an aura
of tension surrounding him. She knew she was
responsible for it, trying to hide her past behind
closed doors. But it still hurt to think about, let
alone talk about.

Hortensia took their order and brought Rick's
Dos Equis and Julia's iced tea. A few minutes
later she returned with their food. The restaurant
began to fill up and she left them alone to eat. The
food tasted as heavenly as Julia remembered from
her occasional meals at the Morales home.

Rick was quiet during dinner. Ominously
quiet, she thought. She chattered, her nerves on

edge. "It's such a small world! Imagine running into the Moraleses. They were our neighbors for years. I used to play with their daughter Carmel."

He gave a noncommittal grunt.

"I don't know how we lost touch. It's been years since I've seen them. I guess I sort of let everything from the old neighborhood go."

"I wonder why you'd do that." He sounded sarcastic.

Julia's mouth snapped shut and she picked at her dinner in silence. She didn't think she liked the direction the conversation was taking, anyway.

Finally they finished. Getting out of the Taqueria was a slow process involving a minor dispute between Rick and Luis, who refused to charge them for the meal. Rick lost, but he slipped a twenty-dollar bill on the table before rising.

Hortensia extracted a promise from Julia to return soon.

"Yes, of course. It was wonderful to see you again and the food was great."

"Make sure you stay in touch now, *mija.*"

"I will. Tell Carmel I said hello, okay?"

She nodded vigorously, then turned to Rick. "And *mijito*..."

"Yeah?"

"You do the right thing by Chulia, *sí?* You know what I'm talking about."

"I always do the right thing, Hope—sooner or later."

He didn't hold her hand on the way to the car.

Julia's nervous tension dissolved into irritation. Wasn't it just like a man to turn and run the first time things didn't go his way? "Are you done sulking yet?"

He gave her a look that would have turned a lesser woman to stone. "I'll drive, if you don't mind." The words were polite enough, but he held out his hand for the keys, a challenging glint in his eyes.

Her first reaction was to tell him to go to hell. Then she sighed. This wasn't about car keys or who drove home.

A few weeks ago she wouldn't have let him in her car in the first place. Now she trusted him enough to hand over the keys if he wanted them, even if he assumed a lot by asking. Why couldn't she also trust him enough to be completely honest with him?

She shook her head, trying to clear it, and handed him the keys. When they reached the car, he unlocked the passenger door and opened it. He didn't wait to close it after her.

As he pulled away from the curb, Julia gritted her teeth. Coming up in half a block was a featured event of this nightmare evening, The Viewing of The House. She closed her eyes. At the last second, she opened them again. Temptation overrode terror. She couldn't begin to imagine why she felt either, but maybe some nice, understanding psychotherapist would be able to figure it out someday. "Stop! Pull over."

Rick's reflexes were quick. He swerved to the side and parked the car. "What's the matter?" Despite the chill between them moments earlier, Julia read concern in his face and voice.

"I just wanted to see the old homestead again." She peered around him. Directly across the street was her childhood home. Or was it? It didn't look right. She checked the number—yes, it was the same small bungalow and the same rundown block.

But the color was wrong. Instead of faded yellow, it was a freshly painted gray with bright blue trim. The porch steps no longer sagged and the lawn was well-kept. Cheery gingham curtains hung in the windows.

"It looks nice," Rick said.

"It does, it really does," Julia said slowly. Then she started to laugh. "Urban renaissance strikes the Mission District!"

"I guess it was different when you lived here."

"Oh yes." She looked up and down the street. Many of the houses were still neglected shacks, but some looked like hers... restored, lived in, cared for. "When I lived in that house, it could have been condemned."

Rick leaned back against the seat and exhaled. He turned off the ignition, then narrowed his eyes at Julia. "Okay. Start talking."

"What?"

"You've been tiptoeing around the subject of your parents for as long as I've known you. You have more secrets than anyone I've ever met."

"Me?! What about you?"

He had the grace to look uncomfortable. Then he grinned. "Yeah, well, I'm holding the trump card here. Start talking or I'll pump Hope for everything she knows about you."

"Cheater," Julia accused without heat. She sighed. "It's not a big deal, it's just not something I like to talk about. I didn't mean to seem mysterious."

"I thought maybe we were talking state secrets."

She gave him a vague smile and shook her head. "When I was growing up, this neighborhood was mostly poor people, single moms, stuff like that. Like the Moraleses—he was a cook at some little restaurant, I think, and they were as broke as the rest of us. It always seemed dreary and—and hopeless around here."

Rick waited for her to continue. She shrugged. "Walking home from school was awful. Carmel and I tried to stay together for self-protection. When we got older, twelve or so, men would follow us and talk dirty, or offer us money to go with them." Remembering, she shivered violently. "I hated living here! You don't know how lucky you were, growing up in that big house on that nice street in Piedmont."

He slid an arm around her and squeezed her shoulders. She blinked, relieved. He might talk tough, but she thought maybe he understood what it had been like for a lonely, frightened girl.

His brows lowered into a deep scowl. "What about your parents? Where were they?"

"No dad. I didn't have a dad, okay?" Julia's face was burning and she knew it. She hated talking about her father, even to Rick. Maybe especially to Rick. "I mean, he didn't marry my mother. I never met him." A thought struck her and she glared at him. "But Mama knew who he was. It wasn't like—"

His mouth twisted into a wry smile. "I'm not questioning your mother's... virtue, so you can calm down. And I don't care if your parents never got married."

"Well, I do." As soon as she said it, she bit her lower lip. "This is hard for me. I'm not used to talking about such personal matters with anyone."

"Tell me anyway. I want to know."

"There's nothing to tell. We were poor. I was unhappy. When I grew up, I swore I'd never live like that again."

"Lots of people are poor, but not miserable. I've met most of the Morales kids at one time or another and they seem well-adjusted."

"And I'm not?" She tried to smile.

"You're doing fine." He picked up her hand and brushed his mouth across her knuckles.

Normally the gesture would have sent a jolt of electricity through her, but she was too caught up in her memories to do more than take comfort from it.

"What did you leave out? Tell me about your

mother."

"She died eight years ago." Her muscles tensed and Rick's arm tightened around her.

"I already know that. How?"

"Cirrhosis." Oh God, she was going to start crying. And she never cried, not anymore. She struggled for control of her emotions. "She wasn't even forty yet."

Rick took a deep breath. "She drank?"

Julia nodded.

"And probably neglected you—"

She flared up automatically in her mother's defense. "She did what she could."

He ignored the interruption. "And I bet you probably had to take care of her most of the time."

"Uh-huh." She covered her face with her hands, her fingers cool against her forehead.

"Your father abandoned her when she turned up pregnant?"

She lowered her hands. "Actually, he didn't stay around long enough to find out about it."

Rick shook his head. "Did your mother work? What did you live on?"

"This and that," Julia said. She laced her fingers together in her lap. "Mama worked as a bartender or cocktail waitress sometimes. Or she collected unemployment or welfare."

"What did you do after she died?"

"I was at S.F. State by then, and working. Afterwards, I just kept on... and then I..." Her carefully-toneless voice broke down. She couldn't say another word without sobbing.

Wrapping both arms around her, Rick pulled her into the warm security of his embrace. "It's okay. You can tell me about it another time."

She bobbed her head up and down, trying for a nod, then gave up and laid it on his shoulder. Finally she felt the tension begin to drain from her body.

"Julia," Rick said tentatively. They were so close, she could feel his voice vibrate through her. "You have to lighten up, baby. This is making you crazy. Let it go. It hurts you so much to wallow in it, and I hate seeing you hurt."

The unaccustomed tears burned behind her eyes again, and she blinked them back. She wanted to say, *I never, ever thought about it until you dragged me out here,* but she couldn't speak. Besides, deep in her heart, she knew it would be a lie.

"Do you want to go home now?"

She nodded wordlessly.

Rick made it home in record time. It was still early evening and he followed her into her townhouse. Closing the front door behind them, he pulled her into his arms again. Julia held on and let him soothe away some of her pain with murmured words of comfort. He patted her back and planted tender kisses on top of her head, in her hair.

She was wrung out from talking about things she hadn't mentioned in years. But somehow, sharing them with Rick made them easier to bear.

She silenced the voice inside her that whispered, *don't forget how Mama always thought life was better when she had a new man... for a while, anyway.*

Julia broke out of Rick's embrace and scrutinized him, wondering. *He's not like that, darn it.*

He met her gaze silently. When she turned away and moved into the kitchen, he followed, opening the cabinet and getting out the bottle of brandy. A moment later, he handed her a small glass of it.

She raised an eyebrow and he laughed. "You're a big girl. I'm sure you can handle it."

Julia stared at the wine glass in her hand, and reached a conclusion as clear and perfect as the fine crystal stem. She knew she could handle more than just a glass of wine. There would never be another man in the world who made her feel like this. Whatever came after she would deal with when she had to. She placed the glass on the counter and turned to him. "Rick."

She could hardly breathe around the anticipation crowding in her chest.

He glanced up from putting away the bottle. "What, princess?" Then he must have read the intent in her face, because he left the cabinet door wide open and reached for her.

With a soft sigh, Julia walked into Rick's arms and went up on tiptoes. His kiss turned her inside out. It demanded everything she felt and craved, everything she had to give. Wrapped in the protection of his arms, she had no more secrets. There was only Rick, and she, and whatever they could share.

She drew back and laid her cheek on his chest, trying to give herself a moment to breathe. His hands stroked down her back and up again, then slid into her hair. But when she raised her face for another kiss, he said, "You know where this is going, don't you?"

She nodded. "Yes."

"It's been a… an emotional evening. Are you sure this is what you want? Because if you're not, tell me now. I only have so much self-control. It's been wearing pretty thin lately."

Through his shirt she felt his racing heart, his tight muscles, and she could hardly believe she was responsible for that intense reaction.

"Yes," she whispered. "I know what I'm doing, and I want you… need you. Stay with me tonight. Please."

His groan was heartfelt. "You don't have to ask twice."

In response, Julia took his hand and kissed it, ruffling the sprinkle of dark hair across the back, then pulled him down the stairs to her bedroom. She turned to him, suddenly anxious. "It's been, well, sort of a long time. What if… what if I don't know how to do it right?"

Rick smiled. "Sweetheart, do you remember Friday night?"

She nodded, biting her lower lip.

"You'll know how to do it right. Trust me." He reached for her and undid the buttons of her shirt, one by one.

Halfway through, Julia stopped him with a hand over his fingers. Waiting was exquisite torture, but she had to know.

"Are you—" She looked away, mortified. Somehow she hadn't pictured all these embarrassing moments. "Are you *prepared?*"

Rick raised his head. Amusement blended in his expression with some earthier emotion. With a gravelly chuckle, he leaned down and kissed her forehead. "I've been reliving my adolescence, carrying them around in my wallet. You've done terrible things to my physical and mental health."

By the time he finished with the buttons and pushed the shirt off her shoulders, she was ready to start on his clothing, too. But he blocked her hands. "No. Let me do this first."

He slid her shirt all the way off and threw it on the floor, then turned her around and unhooked her bra. It followed the shirt. Julia felt her nipples tighten when cool air touched her skin. She crossed her arms over her breasts, but Rick drew her back to face him and pulled her hands away.

"Uh-uh. Let me look. Let me touch."

His words gave her a dash of boldness. "Then let me touch you, too." She grasped the edges of Rick's T-shirt and yanked it up, but he was too tall. She had to let him slip it over his head.

She wanted to stare at him forever. He was

perfect. His hard, muscular upper body was covered with drifts of dark hair, and she stepped forward, nuzzling in it, purring her contentment. She felt a vibration start deep inside him, and she looked up.

It was laughter. She glared at him. He sobered. "I'm sorry. Don't stop."

Her chin shot up. "Never mind."

Rick sat down on the edge of the bed and dragged her into his lap. "I couldn't help it. You looked like such a kitten." His fingers traced the perimeter of her breasts and she shivered. "But now it's my turn."

Laying Julia on her back on top of the bed, he bent over her and drew one ultra-sensitive nipple between his teeth. His tongue brushed the tip. She gasped. Her hands flew up and clutched his head.

"More?" He sounded short of breath, but his words feathered warm air over her taut flesh.

She couldn't string two words together, so she responded by drawing his head even closer to her breast.

"Guess that means yes," he muttered. He stroked her with his mouth and tongue until she was nearly reduced to tears, then he switched to the other side and started over.

Julia still had her slacks and underwear on, but deep inside she felt a creamy dampness building. She drew up one knee and sawed the other against his, trying to pull him closer to the source of her need. He was wearing jeans and she couldn't feel enough warm flesh.

Letting go of his head, she slid her hands between their bodies. She trailed her fingers through the hair on his chest and ran her thumbnails over his tiny nipples. He stiffened in response. One denim-covered knee pushed against her inner leg. Her breath was starting to come in panting waves. Finally she reached his belt, then pulled at it ineffectually.

"Rick. Please."

He raised his head and she saw the barely-contained passion in his eyes. "I want this to be good for you, princess. I want it to last."

"Take off your clothes and we'll go slow. I need to feel you all over."

He attempted a weak chuckle. "If you insist." Then all the heat and hardness of him was gone as he left the bed and unbuckled his belt. Julia pulled off the rest of her clothing with trembling fingers at the same time. She watched him, eager for his return.

Completely nude, he was a beautiful sight. She felt awed by his flawless form and moved by the reverence in his eyes as he studied her body. Then his gaze met hers. He lowered himself to the bed by her side and placed a hand at her waist.

"Julia." Rick drew in a raspy breath and kissed her, deeply, slowly. His mouth left hers and trailed down her neck, then across her shoulders. "I want this to be perfect for you."

She couldn't touch him enough. Her hands

skated over his back, down his arms, across his chest. His skin was a series of contrasts, hard with muscle and bone, baby-smooth in some places, rough with hair in others, warm everywhere. "It is perfect. You're perfect."

As he moved over her, kissing and tasting, Julia's insides turned to warm honey. She could feel his arousal branding her, thrusting against her leg in a rhythmic dance, a burning invitation to paradise.

She slid one foot around his nearest calf. Then her eager fingers skimmed across his stomach and tangled in the thicker nest of hair past his hard, flat abdomen. He made a sighing sound deep in his throat as she wrapped her hand around his rigid male flesh. Her thumb dipped across the rounded tip and came away with a smear of moisture.

Rick's fingers dug into the soft fullness of her hips. "Julia..." Then he pushed her onto her back and slid his hands under her thighs, raising them off the bed.

She didn't understand at first what he intended, until she felt his mouth move almost roughly against her. Then she nearly screamed as she arched toward him. "Rick! Now... I need..." She couldn't speak any more.

He drove her to the edge of another world. Then the magic slowed and stopped. He moved away from her, leaving her in a prison of need. "Wait," he whispered.

She heard him fumbling with the clothes at the side of the bed, and she had to bite her tongue to hold back the words tumbling inside her. *I love you. I trust you. Make me more than I am.*

When he was ready she welcomed him into her body. One hard plunge and he was buried inside her, filling her to the limit, yielding all of himself, body and soul. His groan of pleasure pulsed through her and she wrapped her legs around his back, trying to pull him even deeper. Every fiber of her being strained to give him a taste of what he was giving her. She could feel herself merging with him into a whole that was much more than either one of them.

The waves of ecstasy struck her fast and hard. She clutched at him and cried his name, and he quickened with his own release. They collapsed together in a tangle of arms and legs.

When he could speak again, Rick said as if there'd been no break since the last lucid words they'd exchanged, "Next time. I promise. Long and slow."

Julia would have laughed, but she barely had the energy to breathe. "Rick, it was perfect. I never felt so wonderful in my life." She kissed the patch of flesh that happened to be in front of her mouth—just below his collarbone, she thought—and quivered with an aftershock. "But long and slow next time is okay, too."

❖   ❖   ❖

Rick was wide awake. He eased out of Julia's
bed quietly. She slept, her breathing a rhythmic
whisper. He yanked on his jeans, went upstairs,
fixed a cup of instant coffee, and stood at the
kitchen counter to drink it. After the first sip, he
brought out the bottle of brandy and added a shot
to the mug.

He was feeling a little nervous, that was all,
and it was stupid. But he couldn't remember ever
being so deeply affected by sex in his life. The
whole night had been enough to cave in any
man's sense of self.

He'd gone on a campaign to get her to talk
about her past, hadn't he? Now that she'd finally
opened up enough to tell him about it, he almost
wished she hadn't. The burden of her shared
secrets was more than he'd bargained for.

After they'd made love for the second time—
long and slow and unbelievably sweet—Julia had
started talking again. She'd reminisced about her
childhood a bit, even recalled some happy experiences. Rick had listened, mostly without comment.
He'd kept his opinions to himself. He wasn't
good at talking about wrenching emotions, so
he'd expressed them the only way he could, with
his body. He'd held her and kissed her and loved
her until she couldn't remember the bad any
more, until she could only feel the good.

Afterwards, she'd fallen asleep in his arms,

drained but renewed, too, Rick thought. He tensed
now, reliving the rush of impotent rage he'd felt
when he realized everything she'd been through.
It made him feel guilty for the cushy life he'd led
with parents who never missed a Little League
game, who picked up all the tuition bills without
blinking.

But the worst of it was knowing that she'd
broken down and bared her soul to Rick Perry,
handyman extraordinaire and would-be drug
dealer, when she should have been talking to
Sergeant Rick Peralta, SFPD.

No, that wasn't even the worst. The very worst
was that he *wanted* her to know she was talking to
Rick Peralta, not Rick Perry. It was time to go
back to the original game plan for the undercover
job: get in, do it fast and get out. The rules
applied equally well to Darryl Williams and to
Julia Newman.

*Enjoy it while it lasts, buddy. Because nothing
lasts forever.*

Something tickled Julia's ear. Keeping her
eyes closed, she swiped at it with clumsy fingers.
It came again, a warm, featherweight flutter of
breath, followed this time by the eye-opening
sensation of teeth nipping along the delicate outer
shell of her ear.

"Mmm," she murmured, still groggy. She lay

on her stomach. Rick's long, hard length blanketed her side and back and she curled closer, trying to burrow underneath him where it was warm. He groaned and lifted her hair away so he could kiss the back of her neck. One big hand curved around her waist. She could feel the force of his masculine arousal against her leg. That brought her fully awake.

"Feeling better?" she said, smiling into the pillow. He'd had the nerve to complain, after waking her up to make love at three in the morning, that she was killing him with her demands.

"It's amazing what a few hours' sleep will do," Rick mumbled as he strung a line of kisses down her spine. Each one sent a shiver of desire flitting through her. After he reached the small of her back, he rolled away. Julia felt him tracing the same moist trail with his finger as he said, "Did you know you have dimples down here, too?"

"What?" She heaved herself over. Rick was lying on his right side, his head propped on his fist as he studied her. "I do not! *Babies* have dimples on their backsides."

"This is no baby's body." His coffee-colored eyes darkened as he reached over and stroked the outer edge of one breast. Julia's breath caught when his thumb outlined the dusky-rose circle in the center. Her nipple tightened, straining to meet his caress. Deep between her legs she felt the familiar melting excitement he always seemed to awaken in her.

But force of habit is hard to break. It was Friday, the last day of school before spring break. "Wait, what time is it?"

"Who cares?"

Halfheartedly, she pushed his hand away. "Not you, you do whatever you want, anyway. What time is it?" she insisted.

There was a clock on the nightstand. Rick raised his head briefly, then lowered it. His tongue barely touched the swollen tip of her breast. After eliciting a hungry moan from Julia, he growled, "Six-fifty."

"I have to get up."

"In a minute." This time he drew her between his teeth for one toe-curling instant.

"Ohhh. Rick, I'll be late," she pleaded. Inspiration struck. "I'll have to park—ahhh!—on Eddy." Need for him, need to feel him buried deep inside her, throbbed through her in concert with her heartbeat. She wanted to push him away and pull him close all at once.

"I'll drive you," he said raggedly, switching to the other breast and arousing it to equal prominence. His knee forced its way between her thighs. She could almost feel each individual hair on his leg sweeping across her skin.

She should have been embarrassed, but she wasn't, at how easily her legs parted. He rocked against her pubic bone, his hot, hard male flesh nearly vaporizing her on contact. Her head fell back on the pillow and her breath rasped in her chest. She clutched at his hips with urgent fingers. "Rick, *yes.*"

His mouth closed over hers as he thrust into her throbbing, welcoming heat. He came up for air just once as he struggled for control and gasped, "Oh yeah, princess. I'll drive you anywhere you wanna go."

Chapter Nine

❖   ❖   ❖

At three that afternoon, Rick parked the Porsche as close to Tennyson as he could get. He found Julia's third-grade classroom and poked his head inside. She was talking to a couple of kids while the three of them cleaned up the remains of what looked like an Easter party, but she waved him in. He slipped inside and waited near the door, unsure if he ought to get in her way.

The room looked like most of the other grade-school classrooms he'd ever seen. Still, he was interested in the signs of Julia's personality it displayed. She may not have realized it, but her touch was evident in the current events board, the kids' art exhibit, even the rules for student conduct posted on the wall behind her desk. Her faith in the children's basic worth, and her trust in hard work and honesty, shone through.

He wondered if her students actually absorbed the knowledge and standards she tried to impart. If anyone could give them a decent start in life, he'd put his money on Julia.

The kids pretty much ignored him, but when they weren't looking, she sent him a dimpled smile that started his engine revving again. He winked, remembering the night past and looking forward to the one ahead of them.

"Come on, you, get to work," she ordered. "The sooner we have this place cleaned up, the sooner vacation will start."

An enticing prospect, all right. "Yes, *ma'am.*" He started collecting paper cups and napkins, and turned out to be Julia's most efficient worker.

When the room was tidy enough to suit her, she sent the kids, a boy and a girl, on their way. But as they were leaving, she said, "Kathleen, hang on a second."

The girl bounded back. "What, Ms. Newman?" She gave Rick a shy smile, and he smiled back, charmed.

"I'm just wondering what kind of arrangements your mother made for next week. Do you have some place to go while she's at work?"

Kathleen nodded solemnly. "I'm gonna stay with Judy next door. Mommy doesn't have to pay her till she gets her paycheck next Friday. Judy said so."

"That sounds great. Are you going to have fun?"

"Yeah!" She raced for the door, then turned back. "But I'll still call so you don't get lonely, okay?"

"Okay," Julia said with a grin. "You do that."

After Kathleen left, Rick turned to Julia, laughing. "What was that about you being lonely?"

"Well, with only an eccentric handyman for company, what do you expect?"

He sat down on a table, careful not to tip it over, and pulled her between his legs. "You'd better be nice to the handyman or things might start going wrong around your place."

"That sounds like sexual harassment to me."

"Mmm. I'd like to harass you a bit, sexually speaking."

"Slow down, Romeo. We have a long weekend ahead of us."

"That reminds me. I diddled around with your car this afternoon, and I think you need a new carburetor. I'm gonna take it apart tomorrow and—"

"Tell me on the way home. I want to get out of here now. Nine days of R&R is just what I need."

"Okay." Rick patted Julia on the bottom before letting her go. He hoped she didn't think he was really going to let her get all that much rest.

Saturday morning, a blissful Julia lay back against her inflatable shell bath pillow, surrounded by warm water and bubbles, totally relaxed. Rick had already showered and dressed. She heard him moving around upstairs, no doubt trying to throw together some breakfast, and she smiled. He'd need sustenance after the night they'd just spent.

"Julia!"

"Hmm?" He wouldn't be able to hear her feeble murmur, but she couldn't seem to summon the energy to raise her voice. Heck, she couldn't even open her eyes.

"Oh, forget it." A moment later he clattered down the stairs. "Do you want a cup of coffee?"

She forced one eye open briefly. He stood in the bathroom doorway, two steaming mugs in hand. "Mmm. Yes. Thanks."

After setting one mug on the edge of the bathtub, Rick hunkered down nearby. Julia heard him take a sip of his coffee and then place it next to hers. The room felt misty, warm and intimate. She loved the idea of sharing the space with him.

"You look nice and cozy in there. Want some company?"

Her eyes flew open to see him studying the spot where her nipples rose above the frosting of bubbles. They responded instantly by tightening, and her face heated. She felt exposed, unprotected, but it was an unexpectedly delicious feeling.

Groping under the water, she found her washcloth and spread it over her breasts. "No fair sneaking up on me while I'm still recovering from last night."

"No fair *reminding* me about last night. I may never recover, myself." He reached out and took the washcloth, drawing it along her sensitive flesh as he spoke. Each stroke ignited another pinpoint flame under her skin. "I hope you don't think I can maintain that kind of pace forever."

She gave a purring sigh and closed her eyes again. "Well, you can try, can't you?"

Rick snorted with laughter. After a fond parting squeeze, he withdrew his hand and picked up his coffee mug again. "Actually, I came down to tell you I'm gonna run to the store and get some stuff for breakfast. Your refrigerator is even emptier than mine. Is there anything special you want?"

"Yes. Pick up some more ice cream, please," Julia said dreamily.

He choked and almost spit out his coffee. "Are you trying to kill me? That's *not* the kind of thing you do every night."

"It isn't?" She couldn't repress a grin. "What kind of a weenie are you, anyway?"

"One who doesn't want to give himself a heart attack just yet."

"You know, I've always loved ice cream, but I never had any idea of all the really cool things you can do with it."

"I don't think I want to hear this."

She reached for the washcloth and slowly slid it down the front of her body, into the water. "I mean, it was sweet of you to bring me a dish of honey vanilla in the middle of the night. But then when you started to—"

"Don't do this to me, Julia." He gave her a fierce scowl.

She ignored him. "And I loved it when you—"

"That does it." Rick slammed down his coffee

mug and rose on unsteady legs.

She sent him a guileless look. "Is something the matter?"

"I'm getting out of here before I have that heart attack just listening to you, you little witch. See you later."

"Hurry back," Julia called after him as he left. She lay back against the bath pillow, smiling to herself when he muttered something grumpy in reply and stamped up the stairs.

What a night it had been. Neither of them had gotten much sleep, but then, who needed sleep? After Thursday night, she'd assumed she knew plenty about love and sex... but she hadn't reckoned with Friday night.

Between bouts of lovemaking—*ooh, that ice cream!*—they'd talked endlessly. Lord, he'd even dragged the Danny Spinelli story out of her. He'd treated it like simple, youthful bad judgment, rather than the watershed event it had always seemed to her. And she'd discovered he was right. Once told, the story sounded like nothing so much as melodrama. It had lost the power to frighten her anymore.

The water began to cool and Julia climbed out of the bath. After toweling dry, she brushed out her hair, then headed into the bedroom to find clothes... preferably easy-to-remove ones. When she passed close to the bed, her toe bumped against something firm but not hard.

"What was that?" She bent down and found it,

caught under the covers they'd flung off the bed during the night. It was Rick's black leather wallet. "Oh no. How's he going to pay for groceries?"

Well, it was too late now. He'd probably show up at the door any minute, kicking himself for forgetting it. She laid it on top of the dresser and pulled out her underwear drawer.

Ten minutes later, she'd finished dressing and made the bed. Poppy was outside playing "Kill the Rubber Ball." There was absolutely nothing that required her immediate attention.

Rick's wallet still sat on the dresser. He *hadn't* come back for it. Maybe he hadn't noticed it was missing yet. Maybe he carried cash loose in his pockets instead of in his wallet. And maybe she'd better head upstairs before her baser instincts took over and she opened that wallet to see what was inside…

She couldn't stand it anymore. With a furtive glance toward the stairs, she picked up the wallet and sat on the edge of the bed. She took a deep breath.

He'd pried every secret out of her, hadn't he? Yet Rick himself remained an enigma, ten years of his life still unaccounted for, his activities when he wasn't with her shrouded in mystery, his friends questionable at best. He deflected every question she sent his way. He'd asked her to trust him—and she wanted to—but he hadn't given her much to hang on to besides the force of his presence.

Julia opened the wallet.

The first thing she saw was the lone condom, wrapped in cellophane, that fell into her lap. She smiled. How fitting.

Next was his driver's license behind the window provided for it. *Richard Perry,* with an address on Market Street. His familiar likeness scowled up at her from the hard plastic card. She smiled again.

Facing the license was a row of credit cards in staggered slits. She skipped over those in favor of checking the long back pocket. It held a couple hundred dollars in twenties, and she wondered what he was using to buy breakfast.

Back to the credit cards. She slid the first one out of its pocket, and gasped. It wasn't a credit card, after all. It was another California driver's license.

What's he up to? The questions he'd charmed her into ignoring came back into sharp focus.

The second license was issued to *Richard Bernstein,* at the same address as the first one. The man in the picture, again, was definitely Rick.

Well, he could have changed his name. People did sometimes. But why keep an out-of-date license?

The next pocket provided an even worse surprise... a third driver's license. Julia swallowed hard, trying to stay calm. She couldn't think up a single good excuse for anyone to have three of the stupid things.

This one read *Richard Peralta.* The photo was

him, all right, though his hair looked shorter than it was now. But the address on Vallejo Street was different from the others.

The wallet fell into her lap. She couldn't stand the thought of looking through it any further. God only knew what else she'd find.

No honest person would carry three different driver's licenses. Regardless of what he'd said about not being involved in anything illegal, how could she believe him now? She shouldn't have ignored the warning signs. She shouldn't have listened to her heart instead of her head.

Julia Newman, you've been a fool about a man... again. What an incredible surprise.

She stood up slowly, letting the wallet fall to the floor. Just as she was about to kick it into a corner, a thought struck her. She reached into her nightstand drawer and pulled out a pen, then snatched up the wallet again. After noting down the names and addresses, she stuck the sheet of paper in her pocket.

When she was halfway up the stairs, the doorbell rang. If he'd finally come back now, his timing was impeccable. She raced to open the door.

An empty-handed Rick stood on the porch. "You won't believe this—"

"Forget something?" Julia asked flatly, holding his wallet at arm's length with the tips of her fingers.

He gave her a half-smile. "I got all the way to the grocery checkout before I realized I didn't have any money." Then he looked closer and his whole body seemed to go taut. His sunglasses masked his expression, but his mouth flattened into a rigid line. "I'll take that, thanks."

She dropped the wallet into his waiting hand as if it were radioactive. "You've strung me along long enough. I want some straight answers from you, and I want them *now.*"

"I don't suppose you'd stoop to snooping through other people's wallets, would you?"

"What was your first clue?" Flippancy had never come naturally, but desperation drove her now.

Rick's face darkened. "I can't—"

He stopped speaking and swung away, holding up a hand for silence. Julia thought for a second he planned to just walk away, until a man came into view walking down the lane.

He was little more than a boy, but still one of the largest men she'd ever seen, at least six and a half feet tall, with massive arms and shoulders and huge hands. His hair was cropped short, military style. Not someone she'd want to mess with, even after a lifetime of exposure to the astonishing mix of people likely to turn up in a city like San Francisco.

"Get inside," Rick said without even a glance in her direction. His voice was low and hard. "Shut the door."

"No."

"*Do it,* goddammit, before I do it for you." When she didn't move, he clenched his fists at his sides and snarled, "Have it your way." He jammed his hands into his pockets and watched the man's approach in silence.

"Hey, Freddy," he said as the man reached the foot of the porch.

Freddy grunted something no doubt meant as a greeting. His gaze rested on Julia for a moment. With a nod in her direction, he said, "Who's she?"

Rick shook his head. "Nobody."

Nobody? *Nobody?* Even Danny Spinelli, whom she'd come to think of as the lowest of the low, had loved her in his own way. Now look what she'd sunk to.

"Get rid of her. I got a message for you from Mr. Williams."

"She seems to have a mind of her own."

For a moment Julia thought Rick would let it go. Then he turned and stepped toward her, a resolute set to his shoulders. She might have been feeling obstinate, but she wasn't a complete fool.

After slamming the door in his face, she leaned against it, breathing hard. A second later, she reached over and threw the deadbolt for good measure. Her heart pounded in her chest. Raging pain, fear and fury battled inside her for dominance.

But when she heard Rick's growly voice outside again, inquisitiveness stepped into first place. She turned her head toward the door and listened.

Frowning, Rick turned away from Julia's door.

He was far more concerned with her reaction to his wallet and to Freddy than with whatever show of sincerity that scum-bucket Williams wanted this time. At least she was inside now and out of danger.

"What is it, Freddy? I've got things to do."

Darryl Williams's muscle man never wasted words. "Mr. Williams wants to know if you got the cash."

An instant shot of adrenaline blasted through Rick, and Julia faded a bit in his mind. So the time had come at last.

"You wanna step into my place where we can be private?"

Freddy looked around. There was no one else in sight. "Out here is fine. You ready to make the buy?"

"I have ninety grand. Does Darryl have four kilos for me, like he said?"

Freddy nodded. "Bring the money at eight tonight. You know where. We'll meet you with the stuff."

"Got it." Rick turned away. His nerve endings twitched with excitement, but a yo-yo like Freddy would never know it. Tonight these two were going to be *his*...

"One more thing."

He swung around. "What's that?"

"Your friends aren't invited to this party," Freddy said, his expression menacing. "Make sure you come alone."

"Whatever."

After the man left, Rick headed for his front door. There was a lot to do between now and eight o'clock. For starters, he needed to pick up the money and arrange for backup. And he definitely had to wear a wire, if Williams insisted on meeting him alone.

Then he stopped short as Julia's door flew open. Her eyes sent blue-gray fire burning through him. "You son of a bitch. I should have known."

"You've got it all wrong, Julia." His first reaction was to set her straight. Right now. Whatever she thought she knew, she was wrong, and he was getting real tired of the lies. This business was so close to being finished. What would it hurt if he told her the truth?

"Oh, was he inviting you to tea? Funny, but I thought it sounded like a drug deal."

Rick hesitated, torn. By ten tonight, he'd be able to tell her everything without abandoning departmental practice or his own code of honor. And if by any chance Williams got nervous and called off the buy, no one could blame Julia for what she didn't know. He didn't doubt for a second that should a question arise, someone would dig up the Spinelli case and blow her part in it completely out of proportion. "Could we hold off on this conversation until later? I have to go out now, but I can stop by late tonight. Wait up for me, okay?"

"Is it or isn't it a drug deal you two just set up?"

"You've got it all wrong. Can you just sit tight until—"

"Forget it. You must think I'm crazy. Stay the hell away from me." Hands on her hips, she sent him a contemptuous look. "And be grateful I only heard when, not where."

She stepped back and slammed the door again. Rick swore under his breath and took a step toward the door, then stopped.

All he wanted was for Julia not to have to suffer over this. But he'd be a damn fool to screw up everything over wacked-out hormones, when all he really had to do was wait. Soon, very soon, he could explain.

A drug deal. He could deny it all he wanted, but she knew better. It was every bit as bad as her worst fears, the ones she'd shrugged aside so easily.

Julia didn't move until she heard Rick's door close. Then she sank to the floor and wrapped her arms around her legs. Laying her head on top of her knees, she waited for the numbness to wear off. If only she could cry, maybe it would help. Blinding grief surged in to fill the empty space inside her. It was going to be bad, really, really bad, this time around.

At nineteen, she hadn't thought she'd survive learning about Danny's criminal career. She was older, stronger, more experienced now... and it hurt even worse. Remembering the contentment of lying in Rick's arms after a night of love, she wondered how he could climb out of her bed and betray her the way he'd just done. He knew—he had to know—the devastation he was dealing her.

A strangled sob escaped her, but her eyes remained dry.

Rick was unpredictable. She'd found it an oddly appealing trait. But this she couldn't forgive. *Don't forget how low Mama's standards were. I'm not like that. I won't put up with a man who lives outside the law.*

She forced herself to stand up and brush off the seat of her pants. *Keep busy. No use wallowing in self-pity.* In the kitchen she found some dirty dishes and tackled them, grateful for a few minutes' worth of work.

She happened to have a clear view out the window when Rick left his apartment in a hurry five minutes later. He headed for the garage, his back to her. Her jaw dropped when she saw him stick his lethal-looking gun into the back waistband of his jeans. He smoothed his leather jacket over it.

Julia closed her mouth with a snap. *Enough said. Case closed. Now get on with your life.*

The one thing she knew for sure was that numb feelings didn't last nearly long enough. And the pain was going to kill her, if the worry didn't.

She spent the rest of the day in a daze. But when the telephone rang, she scrambled to answer it. "Hello?"

"Julia." Terry spoke her name with such solemnity that her senses flashed an instant warning.

"What is it? What's the matter?"

"I just talked to Paul."

"Who's Paul?"

"You know, my cousin who's a cop. Remember, I called to ask him if he could check out your neighbor Rick—"

"I can't believe you did that," interrupted Julia. "I thought we agreed you weren't going to."

But her pulse rate zoomed. From the tone of Terry's voice, the news wasn't good. Not that Julia needed Terry or her cousin Paul to tell her what she already knew—the man was beneath her notice.

"You agreed. I didn't. Anyway, I thought it wouldn't hurt to see if Paul could find out anything." Terry's voice dropped low. "He's no good, Jules. You have to stay away from him."

In spite of the fact that she wasn't interested, Julia couldn't help herself. "Okay, what did he say?"

"His exact words were, 'Tell her to stay the hell out of his way.'"

Julia's tongue went numb, but she forced the words out anyway. "Why? What did he do?"

"Paul wouldn't tell me anything else. It must be pretty bad."

"Yes… I guess so."

She hung up the phone feeling even worse. Rick must have had run-ins with the law in the

past. On impulse, she reached into her pocket and
came up with the list of his different names and
addresses. It only took her a second to make up
her mind.

Twenty minutes later Julia was driving past the
address on Market Street that had appeared on
two of his licenses. It turned out to be a private
mailbox place. The apartment number must really
be a box number.

She cut over to Van Ness and headed north.
When she reached the Vallejo Street address, she
double-parked and stared. This was no drop-box
kind of thing. It was a stately, stone-fronted
building that looked as though it dated from the
twenties, the kind that usually housed pricey
condos these days. Was it remotely possible Rick
had ever lived in this beautiful place?

Julia arrived home even more confused, more
depressed, than when she'd left. She went to bed
early, thinking if she was asleep she wouldn't
have to listen to the constant recriminations in her
head. Instead, she had to listen to a woman's
voice coming through the wall from Rick's bedroom at midnight. *Now what?* She buried her
head under the pillow and prayed for him to move
out soon. Sleep was elusive, but finally she found
oblivion.

She slept in on Sunday, waking to find herself
clinging to the curled-up Poppy. Her eyes felt
gritty and her head hurt. She slid into her robe and
slippers and went outside to get the newspaper. It

was at the bottom of the steps. On the way back up she glared at Rick's door. *Low-life. Heel.* She ended up biting her lip in regret. Much as she wanted to hate him, she couldn't. If only he'd turned out to be honest, trustworthy, a real man…

Sipping a cup of coffee, she glanced at the front page, skimming over reports on another tax increase and a Third World political upheaval. The words *Drug Bust* in a headline near the bottom of the page caught her eye. With trembling fingers, she spread the paper out and looked again. *Cop Shot as Bust Turns Sour,* it screamed. A smaller headline beneath it announced *Alleged Drug King Arrested.*

Lord, please don't let Rick be involved in this. Julia's heart pounded in her ears as she started to read.

Chapter Ten

❖   ❖   ❖

An undercover police operation came to a bloody conclusion Saturday night when a San Francisco officer was shot during a "routine" transaction with suspected drug kingpin Darryl Williams. According to Lt. Ray Milano, Williams, now in police custody, agreed to sell several kilograms of cocaine to the undercover vice officer. But Williams apparently planned to rob and kill him instead, causing a confrontation with police in the alley behind Shelby's Grill, a Noe Valley restaurant and bar.

Julia's vision swam. Vice officer? Williams? Shelby's? She took a deep breath and forced her eyes to focus on the page.

Violence erupted when Williams, 26, and an associate, Frederick Henderson, 19, allegedly threatened Sgt. Richard Peralta with guns and demanded...

SFPD Sergeant Richard Peralta? Perry, Bernstein and Peralta... but cop or no cop, he'd lied to her. From beginning to end and many times in between. Well, that was the least of her worries right now. She skimmed the rest of the article in growing fear.

... The bullet struck Sgt. Peralta in the chest. Officers Steven Casteel and Arthur Franklin, who were monitoring the transaction by radio from a nearby vehicle, arrived on the scene almost immediately and returned fire. (cont. on page A-12)...

No! her mind screamed. The newspaper fell from her numb fingers. She felt icy all over. She started to shake and a dry sob erupted from deep in her chest. But no tears came. She was too far gone for tears, too close to the edge of hysteria. *The bullet struck Sgt. Peralta in the chest. The bullet...*

Finally she put the knuckles of one hand in her mouth and bit down hard enough to break the skin. She took a deep breath. Then, scrabbling with the paper, she managed to find page A-12.

... officers seized cocaine with a street value of... both men were apprehended at the scene... Sgt. Peralta, 32, was reported to be in critical condition at an undisclosed hospital...

Critical condition. *Critical condition.* That meant he could die, didn't it? Her breath hitching, Julia wrapped her arms around herself tightly and tried to stop the shuddering.

Then a worse thought struck her. This was last night's news. What had happened since the paper went to press?

Please God, don't let Rick die. Please.

She remembered that last argument with him. She'd warned him to stay away from her. He'd wanted to talk to her later and she'd refused. Later... but there wasn't any later. Later he'd been in a hospital with his life's blood draining out of him.

Stop being morbid!

She had to do something constructive, not just sit there imagining Rick dead. She yanked open a drawer, pulled out the telephone book and found the non-emergency number for the Hall of Justice, then pressed the buttons with unsteady fingers.

An impatient-sounding voice answered. "San Francisco Police Department. Sergeant Mallory."

"Hello, this is Julia Newman. I'm..." Oh drat, how should she identify herself? "... I'm a friend of Sergeant Rick Peralta." Well, she was, even if she hadn't acted like it. "I was wondering if there's any news on his condition."

"Sorry, ma'am, but I can't give out that information."

"Oh." As the officer started to hang up, Julia said urgently, "Just a minute!"

"Yes?"

"Can you tell me what hospital he's in?"

There was a moment of incredulous silence on the other end, then he said, "No, I can't give out that information either."

"Can you at least tell me if he's still... alive?" Her voice fell to almost a whisper at the end.

"Ma'am, you'll have to speak to the homicide

investigators about that." At Julia's involuntary pain-filled cry, he seemed to take pity on her. "Okay, okay. I'm not supposed to say anything, but yes, he's alive."

She sagged into a chair with relief and managed a faint "thanks." After he hung up, she tried to pull herself together. Alive. He was alive! A trembly smile lit her face. But she still didn't know where or what kind of condition he was in.

Calmer now, she picked up the receiver and called the police department again. "Vice squad, please."

It was a good bet that at least some of Rick's scruffy-looking friends were vice cops. She'd lay her money on Steel. Besides, he was the only one she knew by name. Struck by a flash of intuition, she picked up the newspaper again. An officer named Steven Casteel had been with Rick when he was shot. Casteel... Steel?

"Vice." It was a man's voice. He sounded distracted.

"May I speak to Steel, please?" she asked, proud of her craftiness.

"He's out. Want to leave a message?"

She was disappointed, but at least she'd guessed right about Steel being a cop. "Yes, please. Ask him to call Julia Newman." She gave the number. "And while I have you on the phone, can you tell me how Rick's doing?"

"He's out of danger, but he's probably not feeling too great either."

Weakness invaded her limbs. *Out of danger.*

Oh Lord, thank you.

"I'd like to send him flowers. What hospital is he in?"

The voice became perceptibly cooler. "I can't give out that information. Send your flowers here and he'll get them."

"Thanks." She hung up slowly. The vice squad might be more casual than the rest of the police department, but even they seemed to draw the line. Well, she'd found out that Rick was going to be okay. That was the most important thing.

The doorbell rang and she jumped, nerves twanging. Then she looked down at her robe and shrugged. Poppy raced by, barking shrilly on her way to protect her territory. In the hallway, Julia had a sudden attack of caution and peeked out the window before opening the door.

A tired-looking Steel stood on the porch.

She couldn't get the door open fast enough. Her fingers tripped over the lock, but finally she faced him. "Where is he? How is he?" she asked breathlessly.

"Guess you heard already." His unsmiling eyes never left her face.

"About Rick getting... hurt?"

"Yeah."

She nudged the growling dog aside with one foot. "It's in the morning paper. Look, is he really going to be all right? That's what they told me when I called your office."

Steel looked disgusted. "They're not supposed

to say anything to anybody. Jee-zus."

"Okay, but—"

"He'll be fine. I just came by to tell you." Julia relaxed for the first time since she'd opened the newspaper. "He's still kinda out of it, but he was mumbling something about you this morning, so I figured I'd better let you know what's going on."

"He asked for me?" A hard lump formed in her throat.

"He mentioned you, along with a whole lot of other babble. Anyway, I thought you'd want to know. I knew you'd see it in the news eventually, and I guess Rick wouldn't want you to worry."

"Where is he?"

"At the county hospital. It has the best trauma unit this side of the bay."

"If I go over there, will they let me in to see him?" After her trouble on the phone with the police department, she wasn't taking any chances.

"No way. But he'll be out in a few days. Why don't you wait till then?"

She brightened. A few days? Then he really was okay. But... "I need to see him sooner than that."

"He has a round-the-clock guard. No one gets in that room except hospital staff, family and police officers."

"Would you take me?" She squelched the thought that she was being presumptuous. After all, Steel had already said Rick hadn't actually asked for her. But she wanted to see for herself that he wasn't dying. She wanted to apologize for the terrible things she'd said to him. She wanted to make sure the hospital staff was treating him right, darn it!

"Me?" Steel was startled. "Lady, I sat in that hospital all night, and I still have to check in at my office, too."

"Please?" she whispered as a single tear ran down her cheek. Her lower lip quivered. The tears had been hovering near the surface for a long time, and she was past caring. If she had to wait till he was released to see him, to talk to him, she knew she'd end up having a nervous breakdown.

"Oh, all right," he said. "I have to take some of Rick's things back to him anyway. Be ready in five minutes."

"Five minutes?" Julia raced downstairs. Carelessly, she threw on the first clothes she found. There was no time to pin up her hair but she ran a brush through it.

She made it back to the front porch seconds before Steel walked out of Rick's house carrying a duffel bag and started to lock the door.

A sudden thought struck her. "Wait!" she cried.

He looked up. "What's the matter?"

"The dog. Shemp. Did you feed him or anything? He must be going nuts."

Steel shook his head. "He's fine. Rick's sister picked him up last night and took him home with her. She'll keep him until Rick gets out of the hospital."

"I'm glad somebody thought about him, poor thing." Then her eyes flew open and she swallowed hard. Last night she'd lain in bed, furious at Rick because she'd heard a woman's voice coming from his bedroom next door. But it must have been his sister, come to pick up Shemp, talking to him.

How could she have been so narrow-minded?

In the car, Steel explained Rick's injuries to her. "He got hit with a .38 caliber bullet. It fractured a rib and ricocheted off, but the broken rib punctured his lung. That's what put him in danger. It was touch-and-go for awhile, but once the doctors controlled the bleeding in his chest, he was safe."

It hit her once more that Rick's life had almost been snuffed out. Julia dug in her purse for a tissue. She was not going to cry. "But he really, truly is going to recover?"

Steel looked at her sideways, faintly amused. "Yeah. I promise. Or at least, the doctors promised."

At the hospital, he led her up an elevator, down a dreary hallway and around a corner. A medicinal smell surrounded her. Steel stopped at the door to Rick's room and studied her for a moment. "He doesn't know you're coming."

She took a steadying breath and pushed her hair behind her ears. "I know. It's okay."

"Don't be surprised if he fades in and out. It's the medication."

She didn't reply. He knocked on the door and pushed it open. Beyond him, Julia saw a young officer in uniform sitting in a straight chair. He started to rise, then relaxed when he saw who it was.

Steel tossed the duffel bag to the other cop as he looked toward the bed. "Rick, you have a visitor. I'll be back in a while." He held the door open for Julia, then let it swing shut behind her.

She looked around the room. Yellow-green walls, a few chairs, a big bed in the middle. It was just like any other hospital room. That inescapable hospital smell was overpowered by the fragrance from the bouquets of flowers scattered around. She wished she'd brought some, too. The policeman in the chair watched her, a questioning expression in his eyes. Finally she'd looked at everything else and she had to look at Rick.

She caught her breath at the sight of him. How could someone with such golden-tan skin become so pale overnight? He was still a large man, and he dwarfed the bed, but he looked older and drawn. He lay propped against a stack of pillows, his hair tousled, an IV hooked up to his right arm. His chest was bare, but the left side was a patch-work of bruises and bandages, shaved in parts. A sling hung over his left shoulder and supported his arm. His eyes were half-closed.

They opened and fixed on Julia when she tried to say something. Nothing came out of her mouth but a sigh. The sight of him lying in the hospital bed, a shadow of his usual impossible self, was killing her. She hadn't realized seeing him like this would affect her so strongly. All her usual defenses unraveled in the face of her fear for his well-being.

She cleared her throat and tried again. "Rick... hi."

"Hi, princess."

The endearment and his tentative smile were too much for her. Her control collapsed and silent tears streamed down her cheeks. "I'm sorry," she blubbered. "I never cry. Usually."

Rick looked uncomfortable. "Jackson, could you wait in the hall for a few minutes?"

The uniformed officer rose eagerly. "Sure, sarge. I'll be right outside if you need me." He removed himself from the room and closed the door while Julia rooted around blindly in her bag.

"Julia," Rick began. Then he stopped, apparently at a loss. "Why don't you sit down."

"How can you be so polite at a time like this?" she wailed. But she sat obediently in a green vinyl chair, pulling it close to the bed, close to Rick.

He smiled. "Don't be melodramatic."

"Melodramatic!" Fresh tears started. "You could have *died.*"

Rick struggled to lean toward her. Pain flashed briefly across his face and he fell back on the pillows in defeat.

"Don't do that," Julia sniffled, wiping her eyes. "If you need something, let me get it."

"There's a box of tissues in the drawer there, but I can't reach it." He pointed at the bedside table with a wavering right hand. "Help yourself."

"Thank you." She found the box and blew her nose. The double-whammy of terror and relief might have weakened her self-control, but she'd pull herself together if it killed her. Crying wouldn't help Rick. "I don't mean to make a nuisance of myself. I was just so worried."

"Yeah?" His eyes started to drift closed.

"Of course. Rick, I'm so sorry for what I said yesterday."

He didn't respond for a moment. Then his eyes opened. She watched him struggle to focus on her. "Not... fault."

"What?"

"It wasn't your fault," he said, his voice getting stronger with each word. "Mine. I'm sorry, princess."

"You know, I'm not likely to be nice about this forever. Enjoy it while it lasts."

Rick laughed. Then he stopped abruptly and his face turned even paler. Julia's stomach lurched in fear. She jumped to her feet and took a step toward the bed. "Rick? Are you in pain?"

"I'm okay," he said through gritted teeth.

"Stop being macho. I'm going to get a nurse."

When she started to turn away, he reached for her, groping for her hand. "Stay for a minute." His fingers twined with hers. "Please."

"I think you need a pain pill or something," she argued, clamping down on the urge to squeeze his hand, as if she thought she could pass some of her strength along to him.

"They're giving me something in the IV," he

said. "It's all right now. That was just the first time I've laughed. I didn't realize it would hurt like a son-of-a-bitch." He smiled, but there were lines of strain around his eyes and mouth.

And she hadn't even asked him how he was feeling. "I guess you've been in a lot of pain."

"I'll live."

"I wish I could do something to help. I know it sounds trite, but if there's anything you need, please, let me know."

"Actually, there is something I need."

"What is it?"

"Sit down." His fingers wrapped around her wrist and pulled her closer.

"On the bed?" she cried, scandalized. "No! You're injured. I'll hurt you."

"Not if you sit still, you won't."

It was a temptation. Finally, taking great care, Julia sat down. His long, long legs were outlined by the lightweight cotton hospital blanket. Her hip settled against his and her stomach lurched again, but this time not with fear. *Stop it!* she ordered herself furiously. *This is neither the time nor the place for... what you're thinking.* She was almost nose-to-nose with the bare right side of his chest and she had to force herself to look away.

Rick still held her wrist, and his thumb made little circles in the palm of her hand. She'd never realized the flesh there was so sensitive, and she tried to ignore the jitterbug her heart was doing. He looked drained and exhausted, but he managed a ghost of an appreciative leer. "You look great. You're the best thing I've seen in here all day."

Julia felt warmth seeping through her. She smiled. "You look terrible."

He grinned, suddenly stronger. "You wouldn't look so good yourself if you had a tube draining blood out of your lung."

"Oh my God." She sneaked a look at his chest. The side that wasn't covered with bandages looked healthy enough. She itched to tangle her fingers in the silky black hair.

"It's on the other side, under wraps. I have a nice gash where the bullet bounced off, too, and some bruises," he said. "Wanna see?"

"No!"

Rick groaned. "If you have any feelings for me at all, please don't make me laugh again."

His fingers began to meander slowly up the inside of her arm. A languorous warmth stole through her.

"What I need is a kiss to make it all better."

A smile started inside her. "Oh yeah? Who are you planning to get one from?"

"I didn't have anyone special in mind."

Julia giggled. She felt deliciously wicked, thinking about kissing the immobilized Rick. She knew she shouldn't. What if she hurt him? What if he started to bleed? She heard voices in the hallway, reminding her they were in a hospital, for heaven's sake. But oh, just one little kiss. She'd be in total control of the situation.

She leaned over, brushed his lips with hers and sat up again. "All better now?"

Rick gave her an offended look. "Anyone could do better than that. I'm in a *lot* of pain, you know." He slid his hand up until it cupped the back of her head and pulled her down, stopping when her face came within kissing distance of his own.

"Do it right this time," he growled. The exertion must have been too much for him. His hand fell away and came to rest at her waist.

Julia braced her arms on the mattress to keep her weight off him. His gaze held hers for one timeless moment, then her eyes fluttered shut as she closed the distance between them. She kissed him gently with parted lips. He didn't demand any more than that, and she was sure he was too weak to want more.

"Princess," he murmured into her mouth.

A wistful longing, a desire to just make him feel good for a moment or two, ran through her. Why did this have to happen to him? Careful not to get tangled in his IV, she raised a hand to his right shoulder, the uninjured one. Her lips left his and she studied his face. He gazed back but he seemed to have trouble focusing again. Lord, he looked so tired.

She leaned over again, tenderness welling inside her, and kissed his forehead. "Go to sleep, Rick. I'll see you later."

He closed his eyes and seemed to doze off,

then struggled to open them again. "I'll sleep better if you lie down with me."

Julia wanted to laugh, but she couldn't over the lump in her throat. The man was half-dead and still trying to romance her! "I don't think the nurses will go for that. Just sleep. I'll come back tomorrow."

"Promise?" he mumbled.

"I promise."

She waited to leave until he was sound asleep. Carefully removing the hand still wrapped around her waist, she stood and headed for the door, wiping away an errant tear as she went.

Before she got there, there was a light tap and the door swung open. Steel came in carrying a steaming pizza box. He stopped short when he saw Rick. "Guess you wore him out."

"Trust me, it didn't take much."

"An hour or two ago he was howling for something to eat. I had to sneak this in past the nurses." Steel shrugged. "I suppose he'll still be hungry when he wakes up."

"Isn't he supposed to eat?"

"He can, but he doesn't think much of the hospital food."

"Oh," Julia said thoughtfully. Tomorrow she'd bring Rick a feast. Thank God for spring break.

She had so much more than spring break to be grateful for, she realized suddenly. Rick's life was a gift she'd never take for granted again.

❖   ❖   ❖

The phone was ringing when Julia walked in the house. She dropped her handbag and ran to answer it. "Hello?"

It was Terry. "Julia! Where have you been? I've been trying to reach you all day."

"I was at the hospital."

There was a moment of silence on Terry's end. "The hospital. Then you know. About him."

"Uh-huh. He's okay, Terry! He's going to be fine." She was laughing and crying at the same time. "He's not a drug dealer and he's getting out in a few days and—and I'm so *relieved!*"

She could almost hear Terry's smile over the line. "I feel much better. Julia, I want you to know that I nearly killed Paul when he called this morning. Ooh, I could have throttled him."

Julia sobered. "Why did he mislead you like that?"

"He said if Rick gave you an undercover name, it wasn't his place to blow his cover. He didn't know what Rick might be investigating, and he didn't want to mess anything up for him. But I'm still considering methods of revenge. You can help."

"No thanks, I'll leave that up to you. He's your cousin." Besides, she was in too good a mood to hold a grudge against anyone right now.

"Anyway, when Rick got shot, well, I guess Paul figured he'd better let us know. I'm glad it turned out okay. And Jules, I'm really sorry if I caused trouble between you two."

"No, I think we were doing that just fine on our own."

After she hung up, Julia felt energized. She did some chores she hadn't had time for the past few days. Then she went to the grocery store, came home and started cooking, putting together a meal to take to Rick at the hospital.

When she fell into bed that night, exhausted, she slept dreamlessly for twelve full hours. It was the first really good night's sleep she'd had since... well, since she'd met Rick.

❖   ❖   ❖

There was a woman in Rick's room. Julia stood outside the partially opened door trying not to listen to their conversation. She took a deep breath and knocked, then pushed the door the rest of the way open. Rick glanced up at her entrance and smiled.

"Hi," she said shyly.

He looked much better than he had the previous day, his color good, his eyes alert. "I was wondering if you'd show up."

"Of course." She placed her picnic basket on a table and glanced around at the room's other occupants. Jackson, the guard, went back to his newspaper when he recognized her.

The woman was a few years older than Julia,

pretty, with short hair the same burnished brown as Rick's. She eyed Julia with open interest. "Are you going to introduce us, Rick?"

"Sure. This is Julia Newman. My sister, Mary Ann Reilly. Mary Ann was just leaving."

"I was?" Rick's sister started to laugh. "Guess I am now. Nice to meet you, Julia. Bye." She stood and began to collect her things.

"Oh no, don't let me run you off." Julia was startled. She turned to Rick. "How could you say something like that to your own sister?"

"I'm sure she's grateful for the reprieve. She's been here since ten this morning."

Mary Ann said, "It's okay, Julia, really. I left my kids with a sitter and I need to pick them up. I'm just glad someone's here to take over. Maybe you'll like sitting around with a cranky invalid better than I do."

"Who's cranky? All you've done is complain." Rick scowled.

"Spare me the recriminations, please. You can save them for when the folks come back. Oh, that reminds me. Sam called while you were sleeping. Mom and Dad are totally unreachable for the next week. There isn't even any radio contact where they're staying. So there's no way to get them home right now."

"That's okay—there isn't anything for them to do here, anyway. Why wreck their trip?"

After Mary Ann left, Julia took a bowl of Chinese chicken salad out of the basket and placed it on the rolling table next to Rick's bed, followed by mini sourdough baguettes and a crock of sweet butter. Next came homemade spice cookies. "None of this goes together, but I figured you wouldn't mind. Hungry?"

Rick groaned. "Do you want to know what they tried to make me eat for lunch today? Creamed chipped beef on toast, otherwise known as—"

"Never mind that," Julia said. She wheeled the table close to the bed so he could reach everything, then sat in the nearest chair. "Go ahead and eat. Then…" Her voice faded away as she remembered Jackson sitting in the corner of the room.

"Then what?"

With a shrug, she said, "Then start talking, sweetie."

Rick cleared his throat and winced. "Jackson…"

"Huh? Oh." The guard picked up his chair and headed for the door.

"Take some cookies with you," Julia said.

As soon as Jackson was gone, Rick said, "I had a feeling we were gonna have this conversation sooner or later. You were too nice yesterday."

"I was scared yesterday." Julia shifted in her seat. "You don't really owe me any explanations, you know. I understand that you were working undercover."

He looked relieved.

She gritted her teeth and smiled. "But I would be interested in hearing your version of how I fit

into your investigation. Fascinating topic, really.
Do you always sleep with the neighbors of your
suspects? Does it make you seem like just one of
the guys?"

"I'm sorry," he said stiffly. His face was turned
away now, looking toward the window. "I know
the whole situation looks bad from your point of
view. I hadn't meant for it to go that far, but we
sort of got caught up in it, didn't we?"

"But you *lied* to me!" she burst out. She hadn't
come here to pick a fight with Rick, but once the
fear had subsided, the questions had begun gnawing
at her. "I was getting to know you, but *it wasn't
really you,* was it? I don't know if one damn thing
you told me about yourself is true."

Her spine was stretched tight enough to crack,
and her jaw ached from the tension thrumming
through her. She wasn't going to back down now.
If there was anything real between them, he had
to convince her of it. Otherwise, no matter how
much it hurt, she'd have to make as graceful—and
as swift—an exit as possible.

Rick turned back to her, his eyes narrowing. "I
told you the truth about every single thing I could
without endangering the operation. I didn't like
lying to you, but there was no choice. What the
hell kind of a law enforcement officer would I be
if I went around blowing my cover whenever I
felt like it? I wouldn't have a shred of self-respect
left, and I probably wouldn't have a job, either."

"What about *my* self-respect?" Julia flushed as

she realized how close she was to screeching. "I'm sorry. I understand. But where does all that leave me—us?"

His face softened and he reached out with his right hand. After a moment she stood and took it in her own. He pulled her close to the bed. "No, princess. *I'm* sorry. Sorry for lying to you, sorry you had to find out the way you did. But I'm not sorry for what happened between us."

Her breath caught in her throat. "I don't know what's the truth and what was lies. I don't know what to trust."

"Sit down. Here, not in the chair."

She maneuvered down next to him just as carefully as she had the day before, avoiding the IV tube. He kept her hand in his.

"I lied to you about my job, obviously. I joined the PD right out of college. The handyman gig was a cover for getting to Williams. I've had a condo on Vallejo Street for the last six years. The Porsche belongs to the police department." He gave her a wry smile. "My real car is a four-wheel-drive, so I can get up to Lake Tahoe when it snows. Oh, and I don't have a permit for the gun... I don't need one."

"Is that everything?"

"I think that's the full extent of any... falsehoods... I gave you. Everything else I told you was God's honest truth. And everything we did was personal. It had nothing to do with the investigation. In fact, I should have stayed the hell away from you, if I wanted to do my job right."

"Really? Truly?" He nodded. Julia's tension started to ease away. "Still—it's hard. You aren't the person I thought I knew."

"Sure I am. Substitute homeowning cop for transient handyman, and it's me. What's not to know?" He smiled.

She caught herself smiling back, and meaning it. "I guess I can live with that."

"Gee, thanks." He settled back against the pillow.

"At least one thing makes more sense now."

"What's that?"

"How you could have grown up in a rich Piedmont family and gone to college, yet somehow managed to be such a... such a..."

"Low-life?" Rick suggested, his eyes shining with humor.

"Uh, maybe that *is* what I meant."

"You'd be surprised. Did you know I'm the black sheep in my family?"

"You?"

"Sure. I went to U.C. Davis instead of back east to an Ivy League college like the rest of them. I knocked up my girlfriend and had to get married. Worst of all, I refused to go to law school when I finished."

"That's what it takes to be the black sheep in your family?"

Rick nodded, his face solemn but his eyes laughing.

"Send them out to the Mission," she said, "and

I'll show 'em stuff that'll make their hair curl. Oh Lord, I'm sorry," she added, as he shook with the effort not to laugh out loud.

When he'd recovered, he said, "I wish you wouldn't do that."

"I'll try, but being with you seems to bring out that kind of thing. I can't help it."

"Right, now it's my fault."

Julia stifled the rejoinder that instantly came to mind. He'd suffered enough without her adding to his pain by making him laugh. "Let's try staying with serious topics. Why *did* you become a cop instead of going to law school?"

"Start with an easy one, why don't you?" He winced. "I was never interested in law school. It's like I told you before—classic middle-child syndrome. Had to carve my own path in the world. But police work always fascinated me. It seemed so much more hands-on than being a lawyer."

"That does sound like you."

"The kicker was, I was married. I couldn't fool around with another three years of school, although my folks wanted to pay for it. I really needed to get a job, one I could stick with. Something I'd like and that would be a profession, not just a paycheck. The answer was pretty obvious. I had my applications in long before graduation."

"Well, you've stayed with it for what—ten years now? I guess it was the right choice after all."

"For me, yeah. My wife expected me to go to law school, too, and never really forgave me for not doing it. So she did instead. I put her through." Rick's smile was crooked. "She walked out the day after she took the bar exam."

Julia's mouth dropped open. "No."

"Yep. Don't feel bad about it—the marriage was long gone by then. We agreed to stick it out till she graduated and skip the community-property battles. It worked out okay."

"How can you be so cavalier about it? It must have been awful."

"No big deal." He looked away, avoiding her puzzled gaze. After a moment he added in a voice so low she had to strain to hear, "Okay, it was no day in the park, either. To be honest, it was a nightmare."

"I'm so sorry you had to go through it." She shook her head, still in shock.

Rick gave her a self-deprecating smile. "I doubt I'd be so patient nowadays. This job toughens you up... it doesn't leave you with many illusions. I'm a lot meaner than I used to be. A lot less likely to put myself—my feelings—on the line."

Julia inhaled sharply. Was that remark meant as a warning to her? She didn't like the idea and she shunted it aside to consider later, in private. "I know how that works. When you always deal with the seamy side of life, that's all you ever expect to find. I was so idealistic when I started teaching, but I've learned there are a lot of problems you just can't do anything about."

"You're so tough and mean." Rick snorted,

then stiffened. "Hey, didn't I tell you to stop making me laugh? Come lie down with me. Maybe we can soften up that rock-hard shell of yours."

She'd stopped listening. "Rick, I was just wondering."

"What?"

"About your... friend, Tiffany—"

"Stop right there. Get this through your head: Tiffany is not and hasn't ever been my 'friend.' She's an okay snitch—informant—but other than that, she's exactly what she looks like. I wouldn't touch her if my life depended on it... and it probably would, at that."

"Oh." Julia shuddered. "But you don't think— she wouldn't have—she didn't double-cross you or anything like that, did she? She wasn't involved with your getting shot, I mean."

Rick shook his head. "Right now she's about as popular with Williams' gang as I am. In fact, she's left town. I guess she'll come back eventually when things cool down, but for now, she was smart to go. I'm sure those punks are gunning for her."

"But... isn't Williams in jail?"

"Yeah, he was denied bail. I think it'll be a long time before he sees the light of day. But he has a lot of underlings out there ready to step into his shoes."

Julia froze. "They wouldn't go after you, would they?"

"They wouldn't have gone after me in the first place if they'd known I was a cop. Now they know. They'll keep a low profile."

"But… does that mean you can't be an undercover cop any more? I mean, your name was in the paper."

"We never use our real names when we're working, so there's no need to keep them out of the paper. The problem is TV news interviews. We have to keep our faces off the screen." Rick slowly shifted position on the bed. "I'm tired of talking. I don't feel good. Are you going to lie down with me or not?"

"Hmm. No, I don't think that's such a good idea." She leaned toward him and dropped a chaste kiss on his lips. His grip on her hand tightened, then relaxed.

Julia rose and moved away from the bed. Whether he realized it or not, right now he needed rest more than he needed her. "I'd better go now. But will you tell me more about your job later?"

"What do you want to know?"

"How much time do you have?"

"My calendar's clear for the next few weeks. I'm all yours."

She smiled, warmed by the new love blooming inside her. "I guess I can live with that, too."

Chapter Eleven

❖   ❖   ❖

"I think you'll be able to go home tomorrow," the doctor told Rick on Thursday afternoon. "Everything looks nice and clean right now. I'll want to see another X-ray before I release you, though."

"Fine," said Rick. He hated being stuck in the hospital. Now that he'd begun to hobble around, he didn't want a bunch of doctors and nurses hovering over him. With the IV and the chest tube gone, he was eager for his marching orders. "When can I go back to work?"

"Probably in a few weeks. I'm not going to limit your activities as long as you're comfortable, but you'll want to take it easy for a while."

After the doctor left, Rick considered his immediate future. *Borrrring.* Too bad Julia wasn't for hire as a nurse. He tried to picture her fluffing his pillows and serving him breakfast in bed. Of course, with the perpetual hard-on he had when she was around, she'd never be able to make the tray stay flat on his lap.

He laughed, earning himself a funny look from Jackson, who was settling into his usual chair in the corner. He'd waited in the hallway while the doctor saw Rick.

"Looks like we'll be out of here tomorrow," Rick said. He was amused at the expression of relief that appeared on Jackson's face, replaced quickly by polite interest. The kid was probably dying to get back on the streets, where the action was.

Well, so was Rick. But he'd have to wait longer than Jackson would for that. He didn't like it, but it was better than bleeding to death in the street, which had been a real possibility a few days ago. And at least he had Julia's daily visit to look forward to.

She'd come by every afternoon this week, leaving the mornings for his sister. His pulse rate speeded up now, planning their time together. She'd sit with him, all soft skin and sweet scent, and tease him and make him forget about the hole in his chest for a while.

They'd had two phenomenal nights together before real life had gotten in the way. The memories haunted him every second of every day. He was counting the minutes until he'd be whole again, and he was getting closer all the time.

Almost before he completed the thought, Julia walked in the door.

Her tawny hair was pulled back and twisted up, and Rick's fingers itched to remove the pins one by one. He wanted to watch the silken mass tumble over her shoulders as he ran his hands through it. She wore a filmy gauze blouse floating with lace and a full skirt that fell below her knees. The effect was gentle and romantic, almost Victorian-looking.

It occurred to him that she seemed to get softer and prettier every time he saw her. In the beginning, he'd thought she was cute. Now she looked downright beautiful. He wanted to wrap her in his arms and taste every inch of her. Predictably, his body hardened in response to his thoughts.

He clenched his fists on the bed. He was in no position to be thinking about stuff like that. Every time he moved, the left side of his chest hurt. But at least it didn't blaze with pain the way it had at first, and it didn't hurt to breathe any more, either. He willed his body to relax.

The long-suffering Jackson looked up and saw Julia. He grabbed his newspaper and moved out to the hallway, nodding hello in response to her greeting.

"How're you feeling?" Julia smiled at Rick. "I brought you something to eat."

"I knew I could count on you. And I feel great. They're gonna kick me loose tomorrow."

Her eyes glowed. "That's wonderful!"

He threw his legs over the side of the bed and sat up carefully, wearing only the standard hospital-issue pajama bottoms. "Come on. Let's take a walk down the scenic sixth-floor hallway. I was going nuts sitting in here."

Before she could respond, the telephone rang. Rick groaned. The last thing he wanted to do right now was talk to some well-meaning friend or relative. Julia picked up the receiver and handed it to him. Her fingers brushed his for one heart-stopping instant before she moved away, giving him a small measure of privacy.

"What?" he barked into the phone.

It was his 89-year-old Aunt Bertha calling from Arizona. She couldn't make heads or tails of the garbled story Mary Ann had given her, and she wanted to know exactly what had happened to Rick. And how. And why. And she wanted to know right this minute.

While he spoke to his aunt, he watched Julia. She'd straightened the flower arrangements and removed a few dead blooms. Now she moved toward the window and balanced a nicely-rounded hip on the ledge. He caught his breath as she leaned against the wooden frame, facing him in three-quarters profile. The bright April sun shone directly in the window at this time of day. It created a halo around her. The blouse seemed to float around her sharply delineated curves. He could see every inch of the line from her throat to the waistband of her skirt. He could even see the darker shadow of a nipple beneath the lacy outline of her bra.

No way, stupid.

He must have imagined it.

He closed his eyes, his heart pounding painfully in his chest. Aunt Bertha was saying something but his attention had faded away. Her words hardly made any sense to him.

Oh... my... God. He was going to have a heart attack. He knew it. Julia was going to drive him right over the edge. She sat there innocently, her face averted, unaware that the sunlight was undressing her more erotically than even he could have imagined.

"Richard? Are you there?"

He shook his head. "Yeah... yes, ma'am, I'm right here. They're releasing me tomorrow."

"Speak up, young man, my hearing isn't what it used to be."

Julia stared out the window and tried not to listen to Rick's end of the phone conversation. At least, she tried to look like she wasn't listening. What kind of a person was she, anyway? Maybe she ought to wait outside while he talked.

But she would have liked to know who had the nerve to keep him on the phone with these endless questions. The poor man obviously needed some peace and quiet. Julia was amazed at the protectiveness she felt toward him. She'd never had anyone to feel protective of, so she'd never realized what a ferocious emotion it could be.

She'd never realized how alone she was in the world.

"Mary Ann's going to write you a long letter," Rick was saying. Julia chanced a quick peek in his direction. He wasn't looking at her. He'd leaned back against the pillows and bent one leg at the knee. The telephone receiver was in one hand and he'd rested the other on his raised knee.

She tried not to notice his powerful-looking arms and upper body. Even marred by bruises and bandages, he was glorious. The sun glinted off his hair, playing up the red-gold highlights. His beard needed trimming, but that didn't diminish his attractiveness a bit.

As she watched, he raised one hand to his chest and rubbed absent-mindedly at the edge of the dressing over his gunshot wound. She looked away, nibbling without thought on her thumbnail.

Julia wanted to cry, remembering again how close he'd come to dying. That flesh and muscle and bone and blood, gone forever. That heart and mind and soul, gone. The rumbling voice and the quirky smile and the touch that drove her insane. Cold and lifeless. She bit down hard on her thumb.

She would have felt dead herself, inside. And that was pretty darn scary.

Rick leaned over to hang up the phone. "Where were we?"

"You were getting up. But I brought you a roast beef sandwich. Do you want it now, or should we go for that walk?"

"Neither. I've haven't even been able to say hello to you yet."

A golden wash of pleasure suffused her. When he smiled at her like that, she was likely to forget her own name. "Well, hi. What's new?"

"Let's see. I already told you I'm going home tomorrow. Oh, and the doc says I can go back to work in a few weeks."

Julia froze in the act of rising. "Will you be strong enough? I mean, it's so dangerous."

"It's not that bad."

"You're lying in a hospital bed because of that job, Rick. It isn't what I'd call safe."

"Life isn't safe, baby. But I'm careful. Getting shot was just rotten luck more than anything else."

"How reassuring." She knew she was shouting into the wind. The man she'd fallen in love with was a cop through and through, even if she hadn't known it at the time. She tried to picture him selling life insurance or practicing law. It lost something in the translation. She sighed. "I guess I'll take you the way you are, dangerous job and all."

Julia's quiet voice whispered through Rick, giving him too much satisfaction for his own comfort. He didn't need a computer to figure out he was into this deeper than he'd bargained for. But he wasn't ready to give her up yet. She made him feel too good to think about letting go.

And the closer she got, the better she made him feel.

He stretched his right hand toward her. She moved slowly around the bed, her eyes never leaving his. Then she placed her hand in his. Her touch was like a searing bullet, and he wanted nothing more than to pull her into his arms and kiss her into a mindless frenzy. *Not a good idea, buddy.* Instead, he closed his fingers around hers and said, "Sit."

As Julia slid onto the edge of the mattress, Rick clamped his teeth together.

"Are you all right?" She sounded alarmed.

"I'm okay." He'd forgotten for a moment what it felt like when her bottom nestled up close to his leg like that. Her fingers, still wrapped in his, stroked along the side of his hand, making him catch his breath. "Julia."

"Hmm?"

"Lie down with me."

"Someone will come in and see us."

"Who cares?" he said impatiently.

"I do. Your friends are in and out of here all the time. So are the doctors and nurses. I'd be... mortified."

"So we'll lock the door."

"Hospital doors don't lock," she said with a sassy grin. But her fingers moved sinuously between his, and when he drew in a deep, almost pained breath, she caught her lower lip with her teeth.

"Oh, for Pete's sake." He shook his head. Suddenly he felt as though his very life depended on Julia stretching out alongside him, holding him in her arms, filling him with her nearness. "Just sit still for a minute."

Rick's feet hit the floor harder than they had since before he was shot. He headed straight for the door, nearly unaware of the twinges in his chest. Sticking his head out into the hallway, he found Jackson. "I'm closing the door. Don't let *anybody* in, not the doctor, not even the mayor. Got it?"

Jackson grinned. "Sure thing, sarge."

"And wipe that smile off your face, kid." But he couldn't help grinning back.

For good measure, he slid a chair under the door handle. It wouldn't keep anyone out, but it might make them stop and think. He wanted Julia relaxed in his arms, not so tense that she couldn't enjoy the feel of her body wrapped around his.

He returned to the bed feeling proud of American ingenuity. Julia's shocked face greeted him. "What are you doing? Now he probably thinks that you're… I'm…"

"What?" he asked, his interest perking up.

"That we're… oh, you know."

Rick tried to look serious. "He wouldn't dare," he said in his deepest voice as he sat on the edge of the bed. "Come on, Julia, I just need to hold you. Please." He lay back and opened his arms to her.

She kicked off her shoes and pulled her feet onto the bed. Then slowly, gingerly, she inched down beside him. He slipped an arm around her and pulled her close to his uninjured side, her forehead resting against his collarbone. She seemed to be holding her breath, but she let it out and it whispered through the sprinkling of coarse, dark hair on his chest. Her cool fingers slid over his bare stomach until they reached his side. Then they began a feather-like stroking on his sensitive flesh.

Now it was Rick who couldn't breathe.

Julia couldn't think of anything that would feel better than this. Well, maybe one or two things, but they were totally inappropriate thoughts. "Mmm, nice."

She snuggled up to Rick. Heat emanated from him like an over-fueled fire.

"Lie still, Julia. Oh no, don't," he said as her leg moved restlessly against his. His eyes were closed, his face tense. But his left hand slid around her waist, his fingers fanning across the small of her back, holding her tightly against him.

"Sorry," Julia muttered. She tried not to move. Of course, that involved leaving one leg bent over his. Lord, it felt good. A terrible, wonderful heat was building deep inside her and there was a roaring in her head. She hid her burning face in his broad, warm chest.

Lying motionless didn't help, she discovered during the next few minutes. Her heart still pounded in her ears and she had to struggle to breathe evenly. Worse, the urge to run her hands over his body, to taste him, to get inside him, was stronger than ever. And the man hadn't even kissed her.

Yet.

She raised her head and eyed Rick speculatively. This felt so good that a kiss or two could only make it better. When was the last time they'd shared a really soul-searing kiss? But of course, he wasn't quite himself yet. Would he object to a little... well, necking?

Rick opened one espresso-colored eye. Then he opened the other. Julia's gaze never left his as she reached up and pulled the pins out of her hair. She shook her head and thick waves cascaded around her shoulders.

"I wanted to do that," he said huskily. One hand wove into her hair and tightened at her nape.

"Rick." She stopped and cleared her throat. "I've tried, I really have, but I just can't stop thinking about... you know, before you got hurt, and those nights we—"

"Stop. Don't do this to me, damn it." But he pulled her closer and she knew, as if she could read his mind, what he wanted. It was exactly what she wanted.

For the first time in her life, she felt bold and brazen—and it wasn't a bad feeling at all. It was one-hundred-percent purely female and seductive. She smiled. Her fingers grazed the tiny nub of his right nipple as she pushed herself up, closer to his face. Then she bent her head and kissed him once, tenderly, right where his neck joined his shoulder. His skin felt like warm velvet over hardened steel. She wanted to brush the ends of his hair out of the way and plant kisses all along his shoulder.

Rick groaned. "You have the world's worst

timing."

"I'll stop," she said contritely, and started to pull away. He held her immobile. "No. Stay." Turning his head toward her, he gazed at her face for a moment. His left hand came up and traced the line of her cheek and chin, his thumb skimming her lower lip. "So beautiful."

Julia's stomach lurched. She knew she was presentable, but no man had ever told her she was beautiful before and certainly not with such an intense look in his eyes. "So are you."

She meant it. Plus he was honorable, funny, brave and strong, and a whole lot of other stuff besides. She loved him. She knew she'd never stop loving him. The thought made her shiver with anticipation and Rick's arm tightened around her.

When he pulled her head toward him, her lips parted and met his. All her unspoken emotion poured into the kiss. Her tongue touched his and danced away, then skimmed across his straight white teeth. He held her mouth to his as if he'd never let anything come between, nipping at her lower lip. Sensation shot through her like a flash fire and she welcomed the invasion of his probing tongue.

Julia caught her breath when Rick's hand moved down her back and slid over her hip, stopping to squeeze a handful of soft, round bottom. Then, impatiently, he gathered up the flowery material of her full skirt and shoved it out of the way. He smoothed his hand along the underside of her knee, pulling her leg up and over his, just as he'd begged her not to do a few minutes earlier. He might as well not have been wearing the thin cotton hospital bottoms, because his erection throbbed against her sensitive inner thigh. It fed the pounding arousal that clamored inside her for release.

"Can you feel... what you're doing to me?" Rick demanded hoarsely. Julia couldn't respond, not with words, anyway. A wild hunger filled her. But he sucked in his breath as her pelvis rocked against his.

His hand slid farther up the back of her leg, and every nerve ending seemed to flower into new awareness as his fingers probed the elastic of her bikini underwear. They slipped underneath into the soft, steamy curls and when he was at the very center of her being, she almost screamed. But he pulled her mouth roughly onto his, absorbing her, taking and giving and taking again. Now both his hands clasped her hips, hugging them close, and she realized dimly that she was lying on top of him, throbbing against his rigid manhood, her skirt bunched around her waist. Distantly, she heard herself moan.

"Julia... sweetheart." Her knees were wrapped around Rick's hips and he pushed at them, trying to straighten her legs.

"No," she whimpered. She couldn't stop now. Her body was spiraling away from her. She was beyond caring about anything except satisfying the screaming need inside her for this man, body and soul.

"I just need…"

Hazy understanding filled her; he wanted to peel down her underwear. She rolled away. A second later, divested of her panties, she eased onto him again, glorying in the hard, warm feel of his body under hers.

He'd ripped open his pajamas and now he clutched her hips, rubbing against her, seeking entry. Her heart stood still for one timeless moment as he penetrated her welcoming heat, then drove into her hard and fast. She tightened around him convulsively and he groaned his pleasure.

Some wordless part of her brain reminded her to be careful, not to hurt him. She locked her knees around his waist. Her back arched, and she abandoned herself to the mindless ecstasy shimmering through her. *I love you, love you, love you…*

"Baby," Rick murmured raggedly as he shuddered with his own release. He yanked her down and fused their mouths together, but there was no getting any closer than they already were. The fierce intensity flowed between them in an endless circle.

When fulfillment brimmed over, Julia collapsed against him, half-consciously staying to his right. She snuggled in his arms, drained, but more contented, more complete, than she'd ever felt before. This was what she'd been born for… this and *him*.

Rick hurt all over, but it had been worth it. Without opening his eyes, he turned his head just enough to kiss Julia's damp hairline. She lay cuddled up at his side in some misty state halfway between wakefulness and catatonia. He wasn't much better off himself.

She started to stir. "Rick?" she whispered.

"Hmm?"

"Did I hurt you?"

"I dunno and I don't care."

Her smile ruffled the hair on his chest. "And Rick?"

"What?"

"We shouldn't have… but it was wonderful."

He ran languid fingers across her back. "Any time, princess," he mumbled. "Just say the word."

"No, really. I've never felt anything like this before in my life."

"Like what?"

"Oh, you know." She hesitated. "It's so perfect, so right. Almost as if we were destined to be together. I…" She stopped and took a deep breath.

Rick's hand stilled on her back, guessing what she'd been about to say. *I love you.* The words had tumbled heedlessly from her lips as she'd climaxed. At the time, they'd seemed… fitting. But he was wide awake now, tense and alert. It had been more than just the voice of passion speaking, hadn't it?

Women placed a lot of importance on stuff like that. One minute it was *I love you,* and the next thing you knew they were scoping out silver patterns. He'd been down that road before and had no intention of wandering onto it again. It was filled with too many potholes to maneuver safely. A guy could end up just another statistic.

Well, he'd warned her, hadn't he? This wasn't going to turn into something sappy and emotional. And it absolutely was *not* true that at the critical moment, lost in need for her, he'd nearly replied in the same language she'd spoken.

"Let's not make more of this than it is," he said roughly.

Julia's whole body tensed. "And what's that?"

"Great sex. A good time. Sure, I'll be the first to admit it. It's like we were made for each other."

"But?"

"But what? That's enough for me."

"It's never been enough for me." She rolled out of his arms and sat up on the edge of the bed, her skirt fabric bunching in her clenched fists.

She was still fully clothed. Except for the color in her face, the softness around her eyes, no one could have guessed that she'd just made hot, hard, wild love on a hospital bed at five in the afternoon.

Rick flushed. He reached down and pulled the sheet up to his waist. "You knew going into this, I wouldn't be any good for the long run."

"That's what you said before. It just... it

seemed like you'd changed."

The thought flitted through the back of Rick's mind that she was right. He didn't know if it was Julia, the shooting, or what, but his priorities seemed to have reorganized themselves. Maybe— *no way, Jose. Keep it low-key. Are you ready to put your self-esteem on the line for a woman again?* An unreasoning bullheadedness took over. "I like my life fine the way it is, thanks."

Julia stared at him, a stunned look in her eyes. Then, like a robot, she rose from the bed, shaking out her skirt and looking around blindly. She picked up her purse and moved toward the tiny bathroom.

A moment later she appeared again, swooped a hand underneath the bed and came up with a pair of silky ice-blue bikini panties. Avoiding Rick's gaze, she walked sedately back to the bathroom and closed the door. When he heard the lock turn, he grimaced.

Maybe he wasn't as smart as he thought he was.

Ten minutes later, Julia knew she looked as composed as could be expected under the circumstances. She'd straightened her clothes and repaired her hair and makeup. Unfortunately, nothing would fix the turmoil in her mind.

Nothing, except maybe the words "I love you."

She swallowed a sob. Not bloody likely. She'd

pushed Rick into a corner, and he'd set her straight so fast her head was still spinning. Thank God she hadn't broken down and told him she loved him, too.

Her heart had never ached like this for any man, not Danny, not even her father. But she'd trusted Rick. He'd treated her like someone special, made her laugh, forced her to conquer half-conscious fears. And it was almost frightening, the unsuspected passions he'd unleashed in her.

How could she have been such a fool again about a man she couldn't trust not to break her heart? This time, she'd have to pay the price for the rest of her life. Not a day would go by that she didn't think about him, love him, miss him.

Don't forget how Mama always deceived herself about the men she loved. Like mother, like daughter, I guess. Some things never change. Julia bowed her head for a few seconds, praying for strength. Then she looked up and squared her shoulders. She couldn't hide in this ugly fluorescent crackerbox forever.

Better go home, where she could feel sorry for herself in complete privacy.

Emerging from the bathroom, she found Rick sitting up on the edge of the bed, watching her. She stared at the tiny diamond in his earlobe. "I have to get going. Hope you feel better."

He rubbed his eyes with the heels of his hands. The gesture reminded her of a small child just waking up, and her first instinct was to fold him back into her arms. But nothing could ever be the same again between them, could it?

"Are you gonna come by in the morning? I'm getting out in the afternoon."

She shook her head. "I can't."

"When can we get together? I'll be staying at Mary Ann's house for the weekend. Maybe you can come for dinner tomorrow night."

"I don't think so."

Rick crossed his arms over his chest. "Did I hurt your feelings?"

"No. It's okay." Julia hesitated, then said slowly, "This isn't going to work. We're too different. Let's just call it quits while we're still friends, okay?"

His brows lowered to an angry V. "That's stupid. We have something special going on here. You said so yourself."

"It isn't going to work. I–I don't want to see you anymore, okay?"

"I didn't mean—"

"No, Rick. I think you said exactly what you meant." Julia glared at him, swallowing the lump in her throat. "Excuse me. I have to go *now.*" She turned and almost tripped over the chair he'd left blocking the door.

He rose from the bed and hobbled toward her. "Damn it, Julia—"

She shoved the chair out of the way, then yanked the door open and slipped into the hall. Jackson was gone; Wong, the night-shift guard, sat in his chair. How long had she and Rick been locked in there together? Her face flamed when Wong grinned at her. Nodding briefly to him, she hurried down the hallway toward the elevators.

Chapter Twelve

❖   ❖   ❖

Julia went home and cried for two hours. She couldn't seem to stop. Rick had broken some kind of a dam inside her. Then she slept, haunted by dismal dreams, and woke up Friday determined not to sink into depression.

It wasn't that easy.

She tried to do some overdue housecleaning, but everywhere she turned there were reminders of him. In the dishwasher she found a coffee mug he'd used one morning. Under the end table in the living room she found a rubber ball he'd given Poppy. Each one brought a fresh assault of memories that made her swallow back regret.

When the phone rang, her stomach somersaulted. She tripped over her feet running to answer it. *Slow down. It isn't Rick, and even if it is, you don't want to talk to him. Remember?* "Hello?"

"Hey, Jules, it's Easter weekend. Wanna hit the sales at Union Square with me?"

"Terry." A slow smile spread across Julia's face. Maybe a shopping trip was what she needed to take her mind off Rick. "Okay, sure."

"I'll pick you up in half an hour."

Shopping turned out to be exactly what she needed. Over a late lunch at Nordstrom's, Julia reviewed her purchases, staggered by the charges she'd put on her credit card.

"Oh well." Terry shrugged. "Think how much you saved. And you'll be gorgeous. That black leather mini-skirt is dynamite."

"I don't know when I'll get a chance to wear it." Of course, Rick would have liked it. Julia's mood plummeted again.

"Save it for something special." Terry pushed her chair back. "Ready to go home?"

Something in Julia's face must have betrayed her lack of enthusiasm, because Terry sat down again and said, "What gives? You've been acting weird all day. Is it him?"

Julia knew Terry was referring to Rick, although she hadn't told her anything about last night's disaster. It hurt too much to even think about, let alone dissect with her best friend. Still, she found herself giving Terry a bare-bones summary of the situation. And surprisingly, when she was done, the nagging ache in the back of her mind seemed less insistent.

Terry didn't make the usual sympathetic noises Julia might have expected. Instead she said, "Why don't you come home with me? I know Mom and Grandma would love to see you. We'll do fun stuff and forget about men for a while."

"I don't know…"

"Oh, come on. You can spend the night and we'll stay up and watch old movies."

"I can't leave Poppy alone that long."

"She can spend the night, too."

"Okay, you don't have to twist my arm." Julia grinned, even though it felt as if her face might crack.

Terry's house was warm and lively, full of friends and relatives dropping in and out. Julia almost forgot about loss, desolation, and Rick for stretches of ten or fifteen minutes at a time. As usual, Terry's mom Silvia babied her and fed her. She and Poppy ended up staying for the whole three-day weekend.

When she got home after school late Monday afternoon, it was the first time since Friday morning that she'd been there longer than it took to pick up a few clothes. She collapsed on the sofa for a nap.

It was a mistake. Four days of keeping herself occupied had only masked the symptoms. Now, with no one and nothing to distract her, Rick once again monopolized her thoughts.

You were stupid to break it off. You could have had him for a while. That would have been worth something. Then you wouldn't be so empty, so heartbroken, right now.

Sure, she answered herself, *and that's just how Mama would have done it, too.*

No, she knew she'd been right to make a clean

break and be done with it, rather than suffer the slow withdrawal Rick was bound to put her through eventually.

The one thing that bothered her was the memory of his gruff, fumbling attempt to redeem himself when he'd realized she was leaving for good. He'd seemed shocked and unprepared. But then, he probably wasn't used to a woman calling the shots. Right?

He'd wanted to talk about it. She was the one who'd refused.

Wishful thinking, she told herself sharply. *Don't give him credit for emotions he doesn't share. Remember how he reacted when you expressed some feeling for him.*

She remembered, all right. If she lived to be a hundred, she wouldn't forget.

Julia picked herself up off the sofa and fixed a quick supper. Afterwards she went to the library and did some grocery shopping. Even though she kept busy, a litany played in her head. *Wishful thinking, wishful thinking.*

Rick swore and slammed the receiver down in its cradle on the kitchen counter of his North Beach condominium. Julia hadn't answered her phone all weekend, when he'd tried to call from Berkeley. Now it was seven o'clock Monday night and she still wasn't answering. He didn't want to talk to any damned answering machine, either. He wanted to talk to Julia.

He wasn't even supposed to drive yet. But if he had to take a taxi over to her place and camp on her doorstep until she showed up, well, he was just about desperate enough to do it. Maybe he'd even take the bus to her school tomorrow and be there waiting at three o'clock when she got out.

He'd never spent a weekend like this last one. Getting a divorce had been a shower of inconvenience compared to this avalanche of misery. One minute he was tooling along, the world looking like a great place to be, and the next minute he was flat on his face in the mud. *What happened?*

Julia walked out on him, that's what.

For the first time in his life, a woman—one woman—had become vital to him. He should have called her right then and there, when he'd figured it out at three in the morning Saturday.

He'd thought she was trying to lock him into a prison cell. It wasn't until she handed him the key and sent him on his way that he fully understood: the only one locking him in was himself. And if he ever got his hands on her again, he was going to make sure she listened to him this time.

The phone jangled, startling him. He grabbed for it. "Peralta."

"Hey, fella. How's that shoulder?"

Captain Mitchell was a little hazy on the anatomy involved, but Rick wasn't about to quibble. "Great, cap. What's up?"

"Couple of things. First of all, I arranged for movers to go in and pack your stuff at the place in Noe Valley tomorrow. The city will pick up the tab, of course."

"Of course."

"And I need you to come in tomorrow if you're up to it. Just for a meeting or two." He explained why.

"At three o'clock? I'll be there. And… thank you."

A slow smile spread across Rick's face as he hung up the phone. So much for meeting Julia after school tomorrow. Once he did catch up with her, though, she was in for a surprise or two.

He picked up the receiver again and dialed, then waited through her recorded message just to be sure. No human response, so he hung up. Either she wasn't there or she was screening her calls.

Captain Mitchell's news notwithstanding, Rick swore more fluently this time.

Julia walked home from the bus stop at four o'clock on Tuesday afternoon. She turned the corner into the drive and stopped dead. Parked in front of her and Rick's apartments was a big moving van. She was just in time to watch two burly men carry the leather chesterfield out of his place.

She moaned softly. Oh, she knew this wasn't

Rick's home, that he wouldn't be coming back
here to live. But seeing the place emptied out
seemed so final. Especially when she had to live
with a decision that made less and less sense with
every second that ticked by.

Julia was sick of trying to persuade herself it
was all wishful thinking. She couldn't let go of
the idea that maybe, just maybe, she'd made a terrible mistake. Instead of falling apart, she should
have been patient. He could change; people did it
all the time. She herself was no longer the same
person she'd been a month ago, walled off from
any possibility of being hurt.

She should have given him the time and space
to come around on his own. Maybe he never
would have, but at least she would've known
she'd tried. It would have been a lot better than
running away, which was exactly what she'd done.

Maybe it wasn't too late. For whatever reason,
he hadn't wanted her to leave. Maybe he'd be
willing to try again if she could just make him
understand she wasn't demanding a commitment
he couldn't give.

With sudden inspiration, she ran for the phone.
She was going to need all the help she could get.

A couple of hours later Julia changed clothes,
so she'd be ready when Terry arrived. Her lacy
pink camisole-style tank top was the same one

Rick had tried to look down the front of the day he'd come over to check out the kitchen light. Her new black leather miniskirt, black silk stockings and spike-heeled sandals completed the look.

She was determined to use every piece of ammunition in her arsenal. And if it took a cannon-ball to get his attention, she was ready to light the fuse.

The doorbell rang and she ran upstairs to let Terry in. "Thank you so much for coming. You know how bad I am with hair."

"I don't think you called me so much for hair styling as for moral support." Terry grinned. "I'm good at that, too."

Twenty minutes later, Julia stared into the mirror in shock. Her hair was pulled back on one side, and hung loose and sexy on the other. She looked like a woman with only one thing in mind. "Wow! You're a magician, Terry."

"I must have missed my calling. Now go knock 'em dead."

"Wait while I do my face, okay? Then you can make a final inspection."

Touching up her makeup was no easy job. Her fingers shook with nervous anticipation and her breathing felt asthmatic, but finally she was done. She spritzed on a hint of the cologne Rick liked best. Actually, her finger slipped and she sprayed on more than she intended, but the excess would wear off before she got to his house. At least, she hoped it would.

Checking the mirror one last time, she was pleased with the results. If Rick didn't want anything to do with her, at least she'd done her best to distract him from remembering it.

It was up to her to fix things now, if there was anything left to fix. She thought about possible scenarios and her throat nearly closed up. Rick could slam the door in her face. He could listen but not be interested. He might not even be there. Upstairs, she twirled for Terry, showing off the new Julia. "What's the verdict? Will he like it?"

"Yeah. Just make sure no one else sees you," Terry said doubtfully.

Julia stopped dead. "What do you mean?"

"I think it might be illegal or something, to wear a skirt that short. Whatever you do, don't bend over."

"You should have told me before if it's too short." She tried to keep disappointment out of her voice.

"I didn't notice. Maybe it just looks that way, with that camisole you have on."

"Rick likes this top," Julia insisted. "I'm not changing it." But she wondered if she'd gone too far. All she'd wanted was to look seductive for him. She didn't mean to look like a *floozy*. "Terry, do you think I look... well, cheap?"

"Keep your coat on. And don't call me to bail you out if you get picked up for indecent exposure." But Terry leaned over and gave her a hug. "Stop worrying. You look beautiful and sexy. He won't be able to resist you." Then she wrinkled her nose. "Julia, what kind of perfume are you wearing?"

"My usual. Just more of it."

"I'll say." Terry laughed. The phone rang and she shook her head. "The machine can pick it up. Let's *go,* already."

"But it could be Rick." Julia pounced on it. "Hello?"

"Hi, Ms. Newman."

"Kathleen? Are you crying, sweetie?"

Terry made hanging-up motions, but Julia ignored her and turned away. "What's the matter? Is your mother home? She told me she was going to be working day shift."

"She's gonna start next week." Kathleen gulped. "But she just called and said she has to work late tonight. Only tonight. She promised." Her voice broke on a sob. "But she won't be home till ten o'clock and I'm, I'm *scaaared.*"

"Oh, Kathleen. Poor baby." Julia was at a loss. What should she do? "I'll tell you what. I'm going out now, and I can stop by your house and stay with you for a while. It'll be okay if I'm a little late for where I'm going."

She heard a choking sound behind her, and she swung around in time to see Terry draw a finger across her throat. "No!" she mouthed. "Tell her you'll call back later."

Kathleen was sniffling. "Really? You'll really come?"

"Of course," Julia said, her voice low and soothing. "I'll be there in less than twenty minutes. Just sit tight."

When she hung up the phone, Terry said fatalistically, "I should have known you'd come up with an excuse not to do it."

"I'm going to do it! I just need to check in with Kathleen. She's all alone. Besides, it's on the way to Rick's house—well, sort of. And a few minutes won't make any difference."

"Right. A few minutes in the Tenderloin after dark. You're a fool."

"It isn't dark yet."

Terry sighed. "Let's get out of here before the phone rings again. It's almost seven already."

Julia locked the door behind them and headed for the garage. Then she stopped and turned back to Terry, sending her a nervous smile. "Thank you."

"Just let me know how it turns out, okay?"

"You'll be the first to hear."

"I should hope so." Terry laughed as she slammed the car door shut. She pulled out of the lane and took off with a goodbye wave.

She'd been right about one thing. The sun had set and the light *was* starting to fail. Julia pulled her coat more closely around herself. It had been a warm day, but the air had cooled fast. She backed out of the garage and got as far as the end of the main drive. Then the car stalled. She'd forgotten all about fixing the carburetor after Rick was hurt. "Not now, darn it!"

The Honda started up again easily. She drove to Kathleen's apartment building—tenement, more like—on the edge of the Tenderloin and parked in a loading zone nearby. *This is no time to be squeamish about breaking the rules.*

The Simmons apartment was on the second floor. Julia tapped on the door. A moment later it swung open, and she was surprised to see Kathleen's mother, still in her blue and white coffee-shop uniform. "Mrs. Simmons! Aren't you working late tonight?"

The woman gave her a tired smile. "I'm so sorry Kathleen dragged you over here for nothin', Miss Newman."

"That's fine, but—"

"I was supposed to stay late, but when I explained to that manager how I just *couldn't* leave my baby alone so long, he said okay. He even let me leave early when he heard how upset she was, and he said I could take it as sick pay."

"It sounds like you've found a wonderful place to work."

"Oh, I have. They treat me real good, Miss Newman. Now I sent Kathleen to bed. She's sorry she bothered you, too."

Kathleen appeared suddenly a few feet behind her mother, peeking around to give Julia a mischievous smile and a wave. Then she disappeared into the apartment just as suddenly. Julia bit the inside of her cheek, trying to repress a grin that was bound to get the girl caught.

With a straight face, she met the mother's eye. "Honestly, I don't mind her calling. And she didn't ask me to come—I volunteered. So please don't be too angry with her."

"No, ma'am."

It was nearly seven-thirty when Julia made it back to her car, and much darker outside. She didn't regret stopping to check on Kathleen, but the need to get to Rick's house pulsed through her as if it were part of her bloodstream. In fact, she'd warmed up so much in anticipation that she was starting to perspire. She took off her coat and tossed it in the back seat.

In a few minutes, she'd be there and she'd know where she stood with him. Her heart pounded heavily in her chest. She had to force herself to concentrate on driving. Franklin would be the fastest way to get to North Beach from here. She could cut over on Eddy.

While she waited for a red light to change, doubts began to creep in. Maybe she was making a mistake. Maybe she should wait and think about it some more.

No. For once, you aren't going to run scared.

The light turned green. Julia stepped on the accelerator, but nothing happened. The car behind her honked. She shifted into park and turned the ignition. The engine caught.

As soon as she was through the intersection it died again. She had the presence of mind to steer the car to the right and park in a red zone. Once there, she discovered that nothing was going to convince it to start up again.

"Oh no," she moaned, her head pressed to the steering wheel. "Why me? Why tonight?"

Raising her head, she glanced around, frustrated. But frustration over a dead car was nothing next to the irrational fear that she'd blown her only chance with Rick. Besides that, she was stuck in the middle of the Tenderloin after dark, just as Terry had predicted.

Julia took a deep breath and held it, willing herself to calm down. There was no point in looking under the hood, since she knew nothing more about the workings of a car than where the gas tank was located. Stomach churning, she wondered what in God's name she was going to do.

Well, it wasn't that long a walk to bright lights and civilization. She could catch a taxi and deal with the car tomorrow—if it hadn't already been towed by then. It was a measure of her desperation over Rick that she wasn't even concerned about a ticket and towing charges. All she knew was, she had to get to him... and *fast*.

Rattled, Julia climbed out of the car and slammed the door behind her. The street was the usual Tenderloin wasteland. There were people out, but no one paid much attention to her. Fog had started to move in and she shivered in the chill air.

Oops. She couldn't go anywhere without her coat, not in this weather, not in this get-up, and certainly not in this neighborhood. She turned back to the car. Then she stopped in her tracks.

Her coat was where she'd left it, on the back seat. Her purse was where she'd left it, on the front seat. Her keys—well, no doubt they were where she'd left them, in the ignition.

And the car door, as always, was locked.

How could she have been so stupid? She wanted to tear her hair out. She wanted to put her fist through the nearest wall. She wanted to…

Snap out of it. Use your head.

There wasn't much choice but to start walking. Sooner or later she'd find a phone booth, and she could call Terry collect to come get her. She set out, wobbling a bit on the spiky heels because her knees were shaking with fury at her own witlessness. A pay phone in the middle of the next block turned out to be broken, vandalized probably. She kept walking.

One block later, she almost walked into a riot scene. A mob had congregated around a police paddy wagon with flashing blue lights. Patrol cars filled the street. A group of women, prostitutes from the way they looked, argued with uniformed officers as they were steered toward the paddy wagon.

Julia backed up a couple of steps. *Perhaps a different route to civilization would be in order.*

She'd never seen a sweep before, but she'd heard about them on the news. The cops cleared the streets of prostitutes by hauling them in en masse for questioning. No arrests were made; they didn't fool around with charges of soliciting or lewd behavior. The women were released in the morning when it was too late to go back to work. The sole purpose of a sweep was to clean up the streets for a night or two, maybe scare the hookers out of a neighborhood completely.

She turned and backtracked to the corner, then crossed the street. Not a pay phone in sight. But there were only a couple more blocks to go. She heaved a sigh of relief.

Before she could even inhale again, a late-model Thunderbird swerved to the curb. She looked up in alarm as it stopped right next to her. The driver was a man in his late twenties who might have been attractive if he'd bothered to shave sometime in the past week. He lowered the passenger window and leaned toward her. "Lookin' for a date, honey?"

Julia glared at him. "Not a chance. Get lost."

He put on the brake and climbed out of the car. She started getting scared and picked up her pace, ready to run if need be. Why had she worn such impossible shoes? Blood pounded in her ears. She pleaded silently for him not to follow.

But his voice came from right behind her. "What's your rush?" He grabbed her arm and whirled her toward him.

Oh my God, oh no, oh no!

She screamed and tried to yank her arm away. But in this neighborhood no one would pay any attention to a random scream or two, and he was the stronger by far.

"No!" She fought, pushing at him and kicking, but he subdued her easily. He tried to make himself heard over her terrified protests and suddenly two words sank into her brain.

"… resisting arrest…"

"What?!" she screeched, and stopped fighting. Her heart still hammered wildly in her chest and she was racked by shudders, but if he was a policeman… "Are you a cop? Let me see your badge."

"No problem. Just stay still for a minute." Holding her roughly with one hand, he used the other to pull a wallet out of his pocket and flip it open.

Julia pushed back her hair and peered at the wallet in the neon glow of a bar sign. On one side was a shiny silver star; on the other, a photo ID card identifying him as SFPD Inspector Arthur Franklin. She sagged with relief. At least he wasn't some kind of a homicidal maniac.

"Satisfied?"

Her head came up. "What am I being arrested for?"

"You aren't. I'm just taking you in for questioning. You may have witnessed some crimes we're investigating in this neighborhood. I'll let you slide on resisting arrest."

"I didn't do anything wrong," she insisted. "You just scared me, grabbing me like that. I thought you were a mugger."

He shook his head. "You hookers. Can't you ever come up with a new line?"

"I am not a hooker."

"Yeah, right. This must be the first time you got hauled in. Don't worry, it's not that bad."

Her jaw dropped. Not that bad? How much worse could it get? But remembering how terrified she'd been a few minutes ago, she decided it could get a whole lot worse. So why worry about a minor inconvenience like being mistaken for a hooker?

Julia said desperately, "I'm not a prostitute, I swear it. I'm a—" She bit her lip and stopped just in time. *Don't make things worse by telling him the truth. Do you want everyone at Tennyson to hear about this? Or better yet, Rick?*

Rick! He would help her out of this mess. At least, she hoped he would. But then he'd have to know about the whole humiliating episode. No, she'd rather die than drag him into it. She was on her own. "You see, my car broke down and I locked the keys inside. So I was just trying to find a phone booth. To call a friend."

"Oh yeah?" He looked around. "Which car is yours?"

"Actually, it's a couple of blocks away from here."

"Right." Quite obviously, Franklin had lost interest in talking. He headed for his car, pulling the resistant Julia along, and opened the rear door. Letting go of her arm, he grabbed a clipboard from the back seat and said, "Let me get some information from you. And I'll need to see identification."

Julia closed her eyes for a moment. "My purse is locked in my car. I don't have any identification with me."

"No ID?" At her tentative nod, he gave a snort of disgusted laughter. "You really are new at this, aren't you?" Then his voice became serious as he added, "If you can't produce any ID or otherwise prove who you are, I'm going to have to arrest you under California Vehicle Code section 40302a, failure to identify yourself to the arresting officer."

Julia stiffened with shock. She tried to protest but no words would come. Would this nightmare never end? Finally she found her voice. "No! Please, you can't arrest me!" she pleaded.

"That's the way it goes," he said. "Unless there's someone who can vouch for your identity?"

She hesitated. Yes, she'd rather die than have Rick learn about this. But would she rather go to jail, too? "I... I know Rick Peralta, the vice squad sergeant. He could vouch for me."

Franklin raised an eyebrow. "Another one of Rick's snitches? He won't be able to help you out anymore, honey. He's off the vice squad now."

Startled into silence, Julia didn't respond.

"Come on, get in the car," he continued. "We're going downtown. You can make a phone call when we get there. Maybe the ride will help jog your memory."

First, though, he pulled a pair of handcuffs out of the back seat. Julia stared at them, horrified. *This is a bad dream. I'm going to wake up soon. Oh, please, please let this not be happening.*

Franklin eyed her for a moment and then mumbled something that sounded like "oh-for-Christ-sweet-sake." He shoved the cuffs in his back pocket and raised his voice. "Just get in. And make sure you behave yourself."

Julia sat in the back seat imagining cold, heavy handcuffs around her wrists while Franklin drove to the Hall of Justice. He kept a running one-sided conversation going. "You're in luck tonight—the paddy wagon's already full. I'll have to run you downtown myself and let someone in the office deal with you. But at least you have the whole back seat to yourself."

"Well, gosh, thanks," she replied. The sarcasm seemed to be lost on him. *Now you've really done it, Julia—even Mama never managed to get arrested.*

She tried to remind herself that this hardly qualified as the worst moment of her life. Tossing back her hair, she straightened in the seat. It was a case of mistaken identity, that was all. It was excruciatingly embarrassing, but easy enough to clear up. She would phone Terry and Terry would come vouch for her. They'd call a tow truck and get her car unlocked and go home, and everything would be all better. Yes, that's how it would be. She covered her mouth with one hand, trying to stifle

something that was midway between a laugh and
a sob.

Chapter Thirteen

❖ ❖ ❖

Steel sat at a scarred metal desk in the middle of a large, brightly lit room filled with similar desks. Photographs of extremely unattractive people decorated the walls. Other vice detectives sat nearby, and there was a constant buzz of conversation and movement.

Julia kept her head down. The fewer people who noticed her, the better. But as far as she could tell, none of them even bothered to glance her way when Franklin dragged her into the room. "Hey, Steel, can you take care of the paperwork on this arrest for me? I need to get back on the street and find D.J."

Steel looked up from the file he was studying. His eyes widened. "Jee-zus." He reached for the phone on his desk, turned away and punched a few numbers. "Good, you're still here. You better get down here right now." Then he hung up and swiveled around to face Franklin and Julia again, his expression grim.

Julia said, "Hi, Steel." She tried, unsuccessfully,

to smile.

Ignoring her, he shook his head. "Nice going, Artie."

"What? What'd I do?" Franklin's grip on Julia's arm loosened and the tension inside her started to ease.

"I told you," she said.

"Told him what?" Steel asked.

"Not a whole lot," she hedged. "But he wouldn't listen, anyway."

"What the hell did I do?"

"Nothing much," Steel said. "Just arrested Peralta's old lady, that's all. Congratulations."

Franklin dropped her arm and backed away. "Rick's going out with a hooker?"

Julia wanted to curl up and die. Steel stood and rested his hands on the desk as he leaned across it. "Of course not. She's a teacher. What's she charged with?"

"Huh?" Franklin said something under his breath and passed a hand over his eyes. "Never mind. No charge. The charges are dropped, okay?"

"I'd say that's the sensible thing to do."

Franklin mumbled an apology in Julia's direction and stomped out of the office.

Steel gazed at her for a long moment. Finally he said, "Sit down."

She felt a boneless relief at knowing she wasn't going to jail after all, and she almost fell into the chair beside his desk. "Thank you," she said, amazed at how calm her voice sounded. "For getting me out of that, I mean. May I use your phone? I need to call a friend to pick me up." She winced, remembering Terry's prophetic words about getting arrested for indecent exposure.

"Sit tight. Rick's on his way downstairs already. He's been in a meeting with the captain and the deputy chief all night."

"What?! No! I don't want him to find out about this."

"Too late now." Steel glanced past her shoulder and Julia's blood froze in her veins. She turned, expecting to see Rick. But it was some other tall, dark-haired man, clean-shaven and wearing a business suit. He stood in the doorway ten feet behind her with his arms folded across his broad chest. She turned away.

A second later she looked again. Her jaw dropped and she rose slowly out of her chair. She tried to speak but nothing came out. Her brain felt full of molasses, thick and sluggish.

It was Rick all right, a nearly unrecognizable version of him. He wore a charcoal-gray suit, a white dress shirt and a paisley silk tie. She'd never seen him before in any but the most casual of clothes, and she was stunned by how attractive he was in more formal attire. But that wasn't the biggest difference.

His hair was short. He'd let some hip young hairdresser loose on it, and it was fashionably styled, cut close on the sides, a little longer in back. It looked darker than she remembered, although she could still see the golden highlights.

His beard was gone. She'd thought it was scruffy at first, then intriguing, and finally sexy, an integral part of the Rick she loved. Here was a different man, one she didn't know, hadn't recognized at first glance, with only a hint of five-o'clock shadow on his face.

His tiny diamond earring was missing. Except for an almost imperceptible shadow in his left lobe, there was no longer any trace of a pierced ear. Maybe she'd never quite adjusted to his having it, but it was part of him, darn it, and she wanted it back.

His eyes were the same. Deep coffee brown, filled now with a question. A question for her?

"Rick?" she croaked. She cleared her throat, searching for something, anything, to say. "You look... different."

"So do you."

More than anything, he looked exhausted, and Julia worried that he'd been overdoing it. He certainly wasn't supposed to be back at work yet.

"I'm putting together an organized crime task force." His smile seemed strained. "It's something I've wanted to do for a long time. The assignment just came through. Along with a promotion to lieutenant."

"What great news."

Palpable tension sparked between them, and the room grew silent as the others watched, all except Steel, who had his nose in a file folder.

Then Rick's gaze swept over her, and his face lightened. "Now tell me what you're doing here."

Reminded of her humiliation, Julia scowled. "I got arrested. There's never a cop around when you need one, and then they're crawling all over the place when you don't."

He perched one hip on a nearby desk and studied her clothing, his face solemn. She saw a hint of laughter begin to bloom in his eyes. "Just tell me you didn't solicit one of the vice guys. Please."

"It's not funny," she flared. "I could lose my job."

"You weren't booked, were you?" He looked to Steel for confirmation. Without looking up, Steel shook his head. "Then it's not an official arrest. Don't worry about it. And if you need a letter of apology from the police department, I'll make sure you get one. But Julia, you were hanging around on the street dressed like that and you can't figure out why some poor dumb cop thought you were a hooker?"

"I told him I wasn't. He just didn't believe me. Do we have to talk about this right here and now?" She knew everyone in the room was listening.

Rick clearly had no sympathy. "Oh God, I wish I'd been there." He laughed so hard he had to wipe his eyes.

Julia wasn't prepared to find humor in the situation yet, but she supposed she would eventually. Still, right now she would've happily throttled him.

Watching him, she was stunned all over again at the changes in his appearance. She knew he was the same Rick, but he looked so different it was hard to remember that fact. She'd had a whole speech prepared. Now she felt unexpectedly shy about delivering it to this new, unfamiliar person.

Something—panic, fear, misery?—burst inside her at that moment. Mortifying tears threatened again. She bit down hard on her lower lip, then stood motionless, her gaze still on Rick.

Before she could blink, he was at her side, his voice a gravelly attempt at whispering. "What is it, princess? What's the matter?"

She barely noticed as he edged her toward the dimly lit hallway. There, he opened a door and drew her inside with him. A desk lamp bathed the room in a subtle glow, and she saw that they were in a small office. As soon as the door clicked shut, he gathered her in his arms.

"I figured we could use some privacy," he said as he reached out and wiped a stray tear off her cheek with his finger.

"Thank you." Sniffling, Julia closed her eyes and laid her forehead gratefully against his suit coat. This wasn't the way she'd imagined their next meeting would be. But it was unspeakably wonderful to be surrounded by his steadiness once more. Her hands crept inside the coat and clutched the front of his shirt, twisting the material in her fingers.

She wanted to tell him how afraid she was, how lonely she'd been, how she needed him and loved him and wanted to trust him. The words wouldn't come together on her tongue, and instead she blurted what all the feelings boiled down to, anyway. "Don't leave me again."

With dawning horror, she tried to pull away. How could she have said something so stupid?

But Rick held on and wouldn't let go. He'd stiffened at first. Now she felt him relax and he spoke quietly in reply. "I never left you."

"That isn't what I meant."

"What did you mean, then?"

"I don't know. Maybe I was wrong."

To Julia's surprise, instead of replying, Rick turned her around in his arms so her back was to him. When his hands settled on her shoulders, she inhaled a jerky breath. His fingers were warm and gently abrasive on her sensitive, bare skin. If he moved them a fraction of an inch, they'd brush the tops of her breasts. Her nipples tightened at the thought.

Stop it!

She wanted to talk to him, not lose herself in some sexual fantasy. And worse, it wasn't only sex. The need for his reassurance and understanding was sneaking up on her, too. She had to force herself not to lean back into the hard, warm comfort of his body.

"Tell me," Rick said, his voice close to her ear, "what the hell you were doing running around dressed like that? It isn't your usual style."

Julia couldn't help it. Her head tilted backwards and came to rest against his chest. Her eyes closed and a purr started deep in her throat when his lips touched her neck, then moved to her ear and temple. A shudder of pleasure streaked through her, but she tried to pull her thoughts together. They had to talk, and he'd given her the perfect opening.

"I was looking for you," she murmured.

His mouth and hands stilled for a second, then his fingers took up their rhythmic kneading on her shoulders again. "Why?"

She drew in a deep breath and said, "I thought maybe we could talk. About us."

Rick's hands slid down her arms with a tingle that left her stomach in the vicinity of her knees. "You had plenty to say the last time. Was there something more you wanted to add?" His voice was low and even, and she couldn't tell what he was thinking.

She forgot the speech she'd practiced, and stumbled over her words. "I wasn't thinking straight then... wasn't being fair to you. All I could think about was that you might hurt me." Her breath hitched in her chest. "I ended up hurting myself worse."

"And hurting *me,* too. Although—"

"Oh Lord, don't say that," Julia cried, and spun around in his arms. She barely noticed what she was doing as she locked her hands behind his neck and pulled his head down. "I'm so sorry..."

Rick stiffened. "Go easy on the bod, baby. It ain't what it used to be."

"Aaack! Oh *no*." Full of remorse for forgetting he wasn't all better yet, she started to move away.

But he pulled her back into his arms and hugged her close, until she couldn't tell where one body ended and the other began. When his lips touched hers, a wellspring of joy burst inside her, so powerful that it filled every corner of her soul. His hands moved up to cup her face, and he made the kiss gentle and lingering.

Afterward, he rested his chin on top of her head, his fingers tangled in her hair. "You know, this wasn't your fault at all. I was the one who did a number on both of us. In fact, I was a total jerk."

Her face was pressed against his tie, but she managed a faint smile. "Who, you?"

"When did you get so sassy? This is serious." He kissed her hair and she melted a little closer to him. "The last few days have been the hardest of my life. I need you like I've never needed anyone before. Ever. Do you understand what I'm saying?"

She raised her head so she could see his eyes. They gleamed with fathomless richness and warmth in the faint light. Julia knew she could drown in that gaze. Long hair, short hair, all the rest of it didn't matter. What mattered was the real Rick inside, and the window to that Rick was his eyes. They said all she needed to know.

She nodded slowly to acknowledge his question and flicked her tongue across her dry lips. Then she spoke the words she'd been terrified to say aloud. "Rick, you should know going into this, I love you. I'm willing to settle for less from you if I have to, but I won't lie about it, either."

A triumphant smile spread across his face and his fingers stroked through her hair. "Then marry me, princess. Don't make me sweat like this again."

"Marry you?" she echoed in amazement. Could dreams come true? Did Cinderella really marry her prince? "Yes. Yes! *Yes!* I'll be the best wife you could ever hope for... I'll make you so happy..." She bounced around in his arms, wanting to jump on him but afraid she'd hurt him again.

"For Pete's sake, Julia." Staggering backwards into the nearest chair, he pulled her onto his lap. She covered his face with light, happy kisses. Laughing, he tried to fend her off. "Wait a minute, there's a condition."

"What condition? I don't like conditions," she said suspiciously. They were nose-to-nose now, her arms wrapped around his neck. She didn't think she'd ever be ready to let go.

"I don't get to act like a jerk anymore, and in return, you have to be patient with me. Trust me." His eyes grew serious. "I mean it, Julia. I love you more than I can begin to say. I don't ever want to see you suffer again, or go through that kind of pain myself."

"Never again, love. I'll trust you till the day I die. But meanwhile..." Julia bent and nibbled softly on Rick's neck. At the same time she slithered one foot up his leg, bringing her knee dangerously close to his inseam.

He groaned. "Don't do that, Julia. We're at the police department, for Pete's sake."

"Why not? You would have done it if you'd thought of it first." She grinned, reveling in the knowledge of how she affected him.

His groan was theatrical this time. "God help me, I've created a monster." He slid a hand underneath her mini-skirt and kneaded the inside of her thigh. "Hey, this skirt is great."

Julia sucked in her breath as the familiar syrupy heat spread through her. "I bought it with you in mind."

"Mmm. And if you have some ice cream at home, all my fantasies will be fulfilled. Come on, let's get out of here. I've been waiting forever."

She hesitated. "Well, okay. But one thing first."

"What's that?"

"My car is parked in a red zone on Eddy. I have to pick it up before it gets towed away or stripped down to the frame."

"No problem, princess. Let's go take care of it." Rick grinned. "From now on, there's *always* going to be a cop around when you need one."

THE END

Dear Reader,

We hope you enjoyed this LionHearted novel. You may have already noticed some differences between our books and many others, beginning with our covers. I was always embarrassed to read books with 'bodice-ripping' covers in public, so I had our team of artists create covers I wouldn't even hesitate to recommend to my male friends.

You may also notice that necessary violent scenes in our novels have been toned down or take place out of view of the reader. I personally enjoy empowered heroines and heroes who show that honesty, integrity, high values, persistence and love will ultimately triumph over adversity.

We have a different vision of what constitutes excellence in romance fiction, and hope you agree. It takes authors with talent, skill, and imagination plus a diligent and caring editorial staff to produce entertaining and memorable stories. And it also takes *you!* Please write and let me know what you like so that we can keep providing quality and entertaining stories. And, don't forget to tell a friend about our books.

Mary Ann Heathman
President & CEO
LionHearted Publishing, Inc.

The LionHearted Story

♥ ♥ ♥

When forming LionHearted, we discovered that approximately 50% of all paperback books go unsold and are destroyed, often being dumped into our oceans as wastepaper. Yet more book titles are being released each month than there is space for on store shelves. As the number of books increases, their shelf life decreases, severely limiting their exposure time to customers, and limited exposure means limited sales and lower author royalties. Also, many books being released now are actually re-issues of earlier titles that consumers have already read.

It appeared to us that there was a need for an alternative approach to the marketing and distribution of paperbacks, and in the methods of author compensation in the publishing industry. So we chose to create an environment where authors can earn better than average royalties and receive them sooner, and readers can turn their romance reading into an income producing activity by simply telling their friends about LionHearted books!

THE LIONHEARTED STORY

How often have you recommended a great movie, an excellent restaurant, a good book, or even a brand name you liked? All the time! But has any restaurant, movie theater or author ever reimbursed you for the highly effective "advertising" you did on their behalf? LionHearted does!

We will publish six new romance titles each month, and readers can purchase the books at discounted prices saving $1.00 or more per book over what they would expect to pay in stores.

Customers purchase their monthly six-pack from the LionHearted Romance Network (LRN), LionHearted's marketing division. Each six-pack will contain an entertaining and memorable variety of romance sub-genres such as contemporary, historical, Regency, time-travel, suspense, intrigue, and more.

By selling and shipping the books directly to our customers, the money that would otherwise be paid to large book distributors, wholesalers and stores can now be paid to you. Independent LRN Representatives can turn a favorite leisure activity from an expense into a profit making business, and write off any business related expenses.

As a LRN Representative, each month you purchase a six-pack from LRN, you qualify to earn a referral fee on the purchases made by all of the customers you personally refer, and on all of the customers those customers refer, etc. extending to five levels of customers.

LRN Representatives are not required to maintain

an inventory, and there are no required meetings or trainings to attend. LionHearted wants you to spend quality time with your family and do what you love most. We hope that includes reading and telling your friends about LionHearted so they can get their own books—and we will pay you to do it!

This marketing approach presents an interesting opportunity for all authors, LionHearted or not. By building a network of readers, authors can now earn more than the royalties on their own books. They can earn referral fees on the sales of LionHearted's books, and those referral fees will not run out as royalties eventually do, they will continue year after year with the release of each new monthly six-pack.

Since LionHearted does not withhold royalties in reserve against returns, we can also pay authors their royalties monthly right along with the referral fees paid to our Representatives.

Our humanitarian project is a literacy video that can teach people how to read in the privacy of their home. One out of five adults in this country can't read, and illiteracy has been found to be the biggest link to the rise in crime. Unfortunately, many adults won't attend public reading programs because they don't want others to know they can't read. Can we really expect illiterate parents to raise literate children?

Whether you are an author, a reader, or know someone who is, we would like to hear from you.

To receive more information on LionHearted Publishing, The LionHearted Romance Network, becoming a LRN Representative, or to request our author guidelines, contact us at:

LionHearted Publishing, Inc.
P.O. Box 618
Zephyr Cove, NV 89448-0618

888-LION-HRT (546-6478)
702-588-1388
702-588-1386 fax

admin@LionHearted.com
LionHrtInc@aol.com
75644.32@Compuserve.com

Visit our Web site on the Internet at
http://www.LionHearted.com

Or fill out one of the information request pages that follow and mail or fax to the above address.

Note:

If you don't subscribe to *Affaire de Coeur,* a popular romance industry trade magazine that reviews novels from publishers of romance, you have likely missed their reviews of our books. They have given LionHearted the highest rating awarded any romance publisher.

Affaire de Coeur
3976 Oak Hill Rd.
Oakland, CA 94605-4931
510-569-5675, 510-632-8868 fax
SSeven@msn.com

LionHearted Romance Network

___ Please send me your six-pack of romance novels for $29.95+$3.55 s/h. I am enclosing a check, cashiers check or money order for $33.50 (+ 6.5% sales tax if purchased in Nevada).

___ Please send me information on how to become a LionHearted Romance Network Representative and earn referral fees on the customers I introduce to LRN.   PLEASE PRINT CLEARLY

Name_____

Addrs _____

City _____

St/Zip _____

Phone1 _____

Phone2 _____

eMail_____

Customer ID# _____
The last 7 digits of your SS# or Employers Identification Number (EIN) if a business.

Bus. Name _____
Required if your Customer ID# is an EIN.

I was referred by:

Name_____

LRN ID#_____

Mail to: LionHearted Romance Network
            PO Box 618
            Zephyr Cove, NV 89448-0618

Or call: 888-LION-HRT (546-6478)

Six-Pack #1
Order all six books for only $29.95 + $3.55 s/h

UNDERCOVER LOVE — Lucy Grijalva   (1002) $5.99

The last thing undercover cop Rick Peralta needed was a tempting but off-limits school teacher poking around in his business. The rough biker low-life was everything Julia Newman disliked in a man. He was dangerous but irresistible. Soon she found herself in deeper trouble than she—or he—could handle.

"Way to go Lucy! You have a winner." —Affaire de Coeur

IF WINTER COMES — Millie Baker Ragosta   (1003) $6.49

Her husband's deathbed confession shatters Laura Fortunato's world and begins a journey of self discovery, forgiveness and the power of healing love. Ian McMurtry pursues the reluctant Laura as she battles the lingering ghost who must make things right before he can go on to The Light.

"Truly remarkable. Charming. A keeper." —Affaire de Coeur

THE MARPLOT MARRIAGE — Beth Andrews   (1004) $5.99

Widow Lady Phoebe Bridgerton wakes up in bed next to her cousin by marriage, the last man she'd ever want to marry. Charles Hargood believes her late husband fortunate to be dead rather than alive and married to her. Caught, then jilted by his current fiancée he now has a new fiancée: Phoebe.

"Pure enchantment from cover to cover." —Affaire de Coeur

THE SIPÁN JAGUAR — Joan Smith   (1005) $5.99

A week before the wedding Cassie Newton is unexpectedly invited by her fiancé to join him in Canada. John Weiss, an insurance investigator, has traced a stolen art object and is in deadly pursuit of the thief. But something has gone wrong with the case, and he fears he might not survive.

"Inventive. Delightful. Bright, witty and loving." —Affaire de Coeur

DESTINY'S DISGUISE — Candice Kohl   (1006) $6.99

Lord John, the earl of Farleigh, never expected to inherit title or lands. He arranges to marry the youngest daughter of a neighboring lord. Lady Gweneth is the eldest daughter, a widow bitter toward men. She saves her younger sister from the warrior's hands by impersonating her sister and marrying him herself. John doesn't discover her lie until after the wedding.

"A deliciously convoluted romance. Believable characters and true to period situations." —Affaire de Coeur

FOREVER, MY KNIGHT — Lee Ann Dansby   (1007) $6.99

It is 1067 and Cameron d'Aberon, a Norman knight, is in service to William. He does not need or want another wife, his first having betrayed him and caused the death of his son. Kaela of Chaldron hates the Normans almost as much as she hates and fears her evil and lustful Saxon cousin, Broderick. Now she is the King's ward. Cameron's duty is to escort her to court where the king will choose a husband for the spirited young heiress.

"Tension filled... pulls the reader forward to the end." —Affaire de Coeur

LionHearted Romance Network

___ Please send me your six-pack of romance novels for $29.95+$3.55 s/h. I am enclosing a check, cashiers check or money order for $33.50 (+ 6.5% sales tax if purchased in Nevada).

___ Please send me information on how to become a LionHearted Romance Network Representative and earn referral fees on the customers I introduce to LRN.   PLEASE PRINT CLEARLY

Name_____

Addrs _____

City _____

St/Zip _____

Phone1 _____

Phone2 _____

eMail_____

Customer ID# _____

The last 7 digits of your SS# or Employers Identification Number (EIN) if a business.

Bus. Name _____

Required if your Customer ID# is an EIN.

I was referred by:

Name_____

LRN ID#_____

Mail to: LionHearted Romance Network
             PO Box 618
             Zephyr Cove, NV 89448-0618

Or call: 888-LION-HRT (546-6478)

LionHearted Romance Network

___ Please send me your six-pack of romance novels for $29.95+$3.55 s/h. I am enclosing a check, cashiers check or money order for $33.50 (+ 6.5% sales tax if purchased in Nevada).

___ Please send me information on how to become a LionHearted Romance Network Representative and earn referral fees on the customers I introduce to LRN.   PLEASE PRINT CLEARLY

Name_____

Addrs _____

City _____

St/Zip _____

Phone1 _____

Phone2 _____

eMail_____

Customer ID# _____
The last 7 digits of your SS# or Employers Identification Number (EIN) if a business.

Bus. Name _____
Required if your Customer ID# is an EIN.

I was referred by:

Name_____

LRN ID#_____

Mail to: LionHearted Romance Network
             PO Box 618
             Zephyr Cove, NV 89448-0618

Or call: 888-LION-HRT (546-6478)

Six-Pack #1
Order all six books for only $29.95 + $3.55 s/h

UNDERCOVER LOVE — Lucy Grijalva   (1002) $5.99

The last thing undercover cop Rick Peralta needed was a tempting but off-limits school teacher poking around in his business. The rough biker low-life was everything Julia Newman disliked in a man. He was dangerous but irresistible. Soon she found herself in deeper trouble than she—or he—could handle.

"Way to go Lucy! You have a winner." —Affaire de Coeur

IF WINTER COMES — Millie Baker Ragosta   (1003) $6.49

Her husband's deathbed confession shatters Laura Fortunato's world and begins a journey of self discovery, forgiveness and the power of healing love. Ian McMurtry pursues the reluctant Laura as she battles the lingering ghost who must make things right before he can go on to The Light.

"Truly remarkable. Charming. A keeper." —Affaire de Coeur

THE MARPLOT MARRIAGE — Beth Andrews   (1004) $5.99

Widow Lady Phoebe Bridgerton wakes up in bed next to her cousin by marriage, the last man she'd ever want to marry. Charles Hargood believes her late husband fortunate to be dead rather than alive and married to her. Caught, then jilted by his current fiancée he now has a new fiancée: Phoebe.

"Pure enchantment from cover to cover." —Affaire de Coeur

THE SIPÁN JAGUAR — Joan Smith   (1005) $5.99

A week before the wedding Cassie Newton is unexpectedly invited by her fiancé to join him in Canada. John Weiss, an insurance investigator, has traced a stolen art object and is in deadly pursuit of the thief. But something has gone wrong with the case, and he fears he might not survive.

"Inventive. Delightful. Bright, witty and loving." —Affaire de Coeur

DESTINY'S DISGUISE — Candice Kohl   (1006) $6.99

Lord John, the earl of Farleigh, never expected to inherit title or lands. He arranges to marry the youngest daughter of a neighboring lord. Lady Gweneth is the eldest daughter, a widow bitter toward men. She saves her younger sister from the warrior's hands by impersonating her sister and marrying him herself. John doesn't discover her lie until after the wedding.

"A deliciously convoluted romance. Believable characters and true to period situations." —Affaire de Coeur

FOREVER, MY KNIGHT — Lee Ann Dansby   (1007) $6.99

It is 1067 and Cameron d'Aberon, a Norman knight, is in service to William. He does not need or want another wife, his first having betrayed him and caused the death of his son. Kaela of Chaldron hates the Normans almost as much as she hates and fears her evil and lustful Saxon cousin, Broderick. Now she is the King's ward. Cameron's duty is to escort her to court where the king will choose a husband for the spirited young heiress.

"Tension filled... pulls the reader forward to the end." —Affaire de Coeur

**LionHearted Romance Network
Representative**

Name_____

LRN ID# _____

Write: LionHearted Romance Network
        PO Box 618
        Zephyr Cove, NV 89448-0618

Call: 888-LION-HRT (546-6478) or
        702-588-1388

Fax: 702-588-1386

eMail: admin@LionHearted.com

Web site: http://www.LionHearted.com

Lucy Grijalva

Lucy has lived in the San Francisco Bay Area all her life. She attended the University of California while working as a waitress at a coffee shop, a job that provided her with a lifetime of ideas for interesting characters. Since then she has worked in the fields of marketing and promotion.

She loves stories about cops. Her husband Bill was a police officer who was shot and killed in the line of duty, and much of her writing has a backdrop of police work. Lucy has two school-age children.

Her outside interests include quilting and needlework, playing trivia games, people-watching and of course reading. She reads a wide range of books, with a focus on romance novels and historical fiction and non-fiction.

Undercover Love is Lucy's first published novel, although she has had articles published in trade magazines in the past. She is currently working on another romance and a mainstream novel about a troubled police officer.

Lucy Grijalva may be contacted by writing to her at LionHearted Publishing, Inc. or via email at Lgrijalva@ccnet.com, or visit her home page at http://www.LionHearted.com/LGrijalva.htm.